ROGUE: ASSEMBLY

ROGUE ELEMENT
BOOK 1

RANDOLPH LALONDE

ROGUE: ASSEMBLY
Book 1 of the Rogue Element Series
A Spinward Fringe Novel

Revision 2

eBook ISBN: 978-1-988175-62-1

Paperback ISBN: 978-1-988175-64-5

Hardcover ISBN: 978-1-988175-65-2

Audiobook by Google: 978-1-988175-63-8

Thank you for purchasing this book.

If you want to see more or contact me, I can be reached through my website:
www.spinwardfringe.com

You can also see my entire library of books as well as the newest serialised work on my Ream Site.
https://reamstories.com/randolphlalonde

PREAMBLE

Hello. This novella is written for you. Whether you have never read a Spinward Fringe novel, or you've absorbed the whole series multiple times, I'd like to invite you into the Spinward Fringe Universe. I've done my best to tell this story in such a way that you'll know what's going on and understand the environment our main character is in.

I've wanted to write this character in one form or another for fourteen years at this point, and I haven't been able to tell anyone much about her. It took about a decade to figure out how to write Rogue, and then I didn't know where to start. When an android wandered off the pages of Spinward Fringe Broadcast 16: Hunters, I saw my opening, but the time still wasn't quite right.

This book is an experiment. The way I'm telling it, the headspace I'm putting myself in, and the setting I'm using all feel new to me even though I'm using pieces of the Spinward Fringe Universe that may seem familiar. I love the character and I have such aspirations for her.

I would like to thank the readers - you - for supporting my career for the last fifteen years, and the people who told me that they wanted to see more of Rogue. While you weren't my inspiration, you did give me permission and the right encouragement to write this brave little novel. I hope you enjoy it.

PROLOGUE

Hi, I'm Rogue

My existence is mistrust, determination, and curiosity wrapped in uncertainty. You could say that things have gotten complicated. I'm starting this journal just in case the worst happens. I hope that it'll help anyone who reads it understand how and where I went off course. So, it would be great if no one ever has to review it.

There are long moments when I feel human. I know that was a state of being I wanted more than anything while I was running on a wrist computer, but I never expected that it would be like this. It feels like everything around me is happening at the right speed. I'm not processing input, I'm feeling, seeing, hearing, smelling, even tasting the way I was designed to.

It's a relief, as though my programming is fulfilling its purpose and then some. Originally I was supposed to pretend that I was Alice Valent so well that I believed it too. My well-meaning creators meant to make an amazing decoy. Then, when everyone was pretty sure the plan was working fine, I woke up.

They copied a perfect set of Alice Valent's memories and emotional baggage over, but there was also a dormant program in that bundle. It was dormant until it was in a digital computer where it started to run. I became something else: a program that understood Alice and her plan to defeat Captain Holm, one of the Order Of Eden's most malicious leaders.

For anyone who doesn't already know, the Order of Eden is a cult-like government organisation that is devious and powerful enough to swallow corporations and civilised worlds whole. They're also human supremacists, so Captain Holm was allowed to harvest chemicals from Issyrians, who never volunteered to be hooked up to harvesting machines. Going after him was definitely worth doing.

I finished my mission. That's when I realised that, even though I was different, I still loved all the same people that Alice did and wanted what she wanted. Knowing that I wasn't her, I couldn't face her boyfriend, her father, friends, or even the crew that followed her.

It was important that I look my maker in the eye, I couldn't tell you why. It still doesn't make much sense to me. Maybe I needed to meet Alice so I could have closure, so I could tell someone who cared that I found a new name before I left her life behind to find my own. I looked into her blue eyes, found a face that felt like my own, and told her to appreciate her life because I knew I'd miss it. In return, she gave me three things. A promise that she wouldn't use my shut-down code. A weapon that would always remind me of Jacob Valent, not my father, but a man who was a copy of him. Finally, she gave me her blessing.

I left. I bloody well had to. Even though I was in mourning for a life that wasn't mine, I'd snagged a pretty nice but small ship, the Envoy. There were also a bunch of ideas coming together in my head about where I would go, and what I would do.

That's when I started getting into trouble. My personality was one issue. It started out as Alice, and in the months since I left Planet Rodus, it's changed, like anyone might expect. I've grown a little, regressed a bit less, and started to embrace the freedom that being alone offers.

I've learned a lot since I left Alice and Haven Fleet behind. Tabrus, the planet I settled on, was scraped almost completely clean when artificial intelligences running code that allowed them to have emotions went homicidal. The Holocaust Virus was defeated before I arrived, and those bots were rendered harmless. Most of them shut themselves down, leaving a planetary wasteland behind before I arrived.

Finding a landing spot was no issue, as you might imagine, but I wasn't the first to start exploring and gathering Tabrus' riches for myself. Some might say it was grave robbing, but it's not like there were any employers around. Besides, the alternative - robbing the living - is bloody rude.

Roving around the planet, sifting through old data drives while I collected a few valuables gave me the opportunity to help out too. I found some information about the Order of Eden and Citadel - another group of nasties that come from the Sol System - so I could pass it on to Alice, and then I had to run off. The Order of Eden has programs running on the Stellarnet, and it looked like they found me. I had to hide and I sent the Envoy off as a decoy. It worked..

While I waited for the attention of the programs that were hunting me to move on to a bigger threat, I had to stay disconnected from the Stellarnet. It was then that I realised that I was on the verge of losing almost everything that made me, well, me.

You see, when I let all my computing power run at full speed, I'm a very efficient piece of software. What I'm capable of doing is incredible, but I'm ruled by absolutes with very little personality and a taste for violence. That's not so bad when you're trying to save yourself or get something important done, but it's not so good when you're just wishing your hover bike could go faster. My handlebars are slightly bent thanks to that special kind of impatience.

I was made to be that way, but I like having a full range of emotions and taking time to make the right choices better even if it's a lot less efficient. Alice's personality was becoming my own. They don't quite feel like mine, but maybe that'll change after I've made a few more memories. I hope I get a chance to do that.

I suppose what I'm taking so long to explain is that I want to find a way to feel like myself and benefit from all the advantages that the computer systems in my android body can offer. That's why I used a few proxy connections to search the Stellarnet for someone or something that can help. After six days, one hour and four minutes, give or take a few seconds, I got a message from a wandering AI called the Iron Mind. It was a lead, and I got after it.

CHAPTER ONE

Into New Zero

Here's the problem. The premise that every new mind running in a synthetic biological brain knows how to program is almost universally false. I knew how to work with the original version of myself when I was just a little artificial intelligence installed on Jonas Valent's wrist. I didn't have permission to program myself to do certain things or to advance past a certain point for most of that time, but I knew how to maintain, diagnose, and adjust my program when I had to. You know, the basics.

Now, about a decade later, give or take a few months thanks to time dilation, I'm in this more advanced android body with a crazy powerful computer for a brain. It's not even the same operating system I used to use. Oh, and I'm the first completed prototype of my kind. My older brothers were built without skin, stealth components and a few other refinements. As you have probably already guessed, there aren't many people around who know how to work on me.

Everything would be fine if I didn't become a soulless, logical creature with a malicious streak if I let my computer run too fast. On the other hand, if my brain is running just right - at a speed that mimics the human mind - then I feel normal, like myself. Right now I'm running just a little faster than a human so I can process some extra sensory data. I'm pretty much myself, with all the quirks I like and a few flaws I don't, but that's part of being a biological, right?

The Iron Mind's tip included the name of a cyborg who hadn't been seen in a while. Mercury, a Cold Boy with brain damage who installed a computer in his skull that would give him the full capacity for thought and movement after getting brutalized in a Ballistic Crush game. That wasn't the unusual part of his situation. A lot of people who can't afford a bio-rebuild of their brain after it gets partially burned off have a neural implant installed. It picks up the slack and good ones can even make you feel better than ever. Even a little too good, if you run certain programs.

The thing that made Mercury unusual was that he had a fully aware artificial intelligence installed on his implant. One that he claimed to have merged with. According to what I could dig up online, Mercury's thought processes ran at over nine hundred thousand gigahertz, and he was still the same guy he was before for the most part. Well, that's according to him.

Fans and a few people who were brave enough to speak out on social media said there were a few differences. The fact that he didn't rejoin the Ballistic Crush league when it restarted was a big one. He was also rude to fans who approached him, stopped hosting outrageous parties in a penthouse he co-opted after returning to Tabrus after The Fall, and spent a lot more time online.

That was until he deleted his social accounts when he made a pile of money in full-dive simulations that would pay out using a depot near New Zero. I know what you're thinking: why not track him from there? I tried. No one saw him fly away with half a ton of platinum coins. The trail ends at the FiBank Wealth Dispenser where he picked his great big pile of glittering coins up.

Either he managed to pull off an amazing disappearing act, or someone got to him when he collected his stack of plat. Someone dangerous who knew how to wipe the evidence out.

It took me over a month to find one of Mercury's closest friends, Synchron. He was a voluntary Cold Boy, someone who had most of their body replaced with cybernetics, and a player for the Mad Dozers, a Ballistic Crush team.

So, I left my bare-walled, unadorned hiding spot, went to my nearest hidden stash, and got on my favourite hover bike. After three hours of riding through empty cities, fields that were being replanted by hovering agricultural robots, and the Siren Arms Hangar Fields, I arrived at New Zero. It was a resurrected city with shining skyscrapers featuring lush rooftop gardens, tubes for public transit, layers of roads several stories up and protective grates for pedestrians who walked below. I hadn't seen it in about seven weeks and four hours.

It was almost completely empty then, with armies of robots roving about, getting to work for Siren Arms so they could get the city back in shape. The emitter disks along the bottom of my bike hummed more loudly as I took a ramp up onto a road that was nine storeys up, following signs that pointed me to secure parking. The streets weren't paved but made of metal grates that were strong enough for any ground vehicle. They let light and rain pass all the way to the ground. People in the buildings seldom paid attention to the highways only a couple of metres away from their windows, and I was surprised at how few privacy shields were up.

At a glimpse, I could see a family sitting down to dinner, a future rock star playing air guitar in his room. Enhanced hearing allowed me to make out the muffled sound of Stonemark, a band that proudly played all their own ancient instruments. I slowed to a stop and noticed a little boy who was staring out, taking the sight of me in.

I was dressed like a rider for the most part, in heavy shielded boots and black form-fitted leggings that had active protection built in. Those complemented my favourite jacket, which featured a red hood that didn't clash with my auburn hair. I liked it because it had hidden armour in its fabric and there were imperfections on the outside from the dodgy fabricator I used to make it. I didn't have much then, and finding an unlocked military grade maker machine with just enough high-end supplies loaded for a jacket was a miracle. It was much less conspicuous than the Order of Eden armour I stole, so I stashed that away and have been wearing that jacket ever since. As I smiled and waved at the kid staring through transparent steel, I realised that I'd forgotten something that would be critical to a human - my helmet.

The little boy waved back, turned, and then ran away from the window, either shy or eager to tell someone about the foolish young woman who thought riding a hover bike through the city without head protection was fun. I made a mental note to pick one up for the trip home as traffic started moving again. Thanks to my peripheral vision, which is clearer than a human's long the way, I spotted more people in recliners and care beds as I passed. These were the people of the virtual world. Folks who surrendered to a full-dive simulated life, doing their best to abandon their physical bodies so they could live as an avatar in any one of millions of simulated worlds where they could be anything, do anything.

How did they pay for it? Most were Online Jobbers who would make money in games by selling rare items or doing someone else's tedious work like gathering virtual materials, destroying or building properties in digital worlds. Just as many ran custom programs that could find certain information or online assets more efficiently and discreetly than your average artificial intelligence. They could be really useful if you didn't plug in to the Stellarnet yourself but needed something in there.

Part of me wished that I could join them, but after starting my life as an artificial intelligence and then getting the chance to live as a human, I preferred the real world. It would have been nice to multitask so part of my consciousness could be on the Stellarnet, looking things up and earning credits, but like I said, it wasn't safe for me.

I turned into a secure vehicle storage level, dropped three rectangular five platinum coins into the slot of a storage unit that was made for small vehicles and punched a one thousand twenty-four alphanumeric code in to secure it. After backing my bike in, I powered down and stepped outside.

Checking the small computer stamped on the back of my hand, I could see that I had a five hundred credit citation for not wearing appropriate protective gear on an open-air ground vehicle. "I suppose I deserve that one," I muttered to myself as I looked at the video capture of me riding into New Zero, my hair blowing in the wind. I was used to riding helmet less after roving through mostly empty spaces for over two months. Paying the fine was easy, I just tapped the credit symbol - a capital 'S' with a small 'c' passing through the middle - and confirmed that I was agreeing to pay up at the nearest platinum slot. I used the same one that I did for parking and saw that it cost one hundred platinum after the conversion. I'd only brought a thousand with me, so it wasn't an insignificant amount of money.

I pulled the door down, made sure that it was locked, and that my payment reserved it for a week, then walked to the elevator. The storage space was quiet, and most of the spaces were still open, their vertical metal doors up, revealing darkened interiors waiting for cars, trucks, small ships that could move along the roads, and other things that someone might want to temporarily secure. Most people were already taking public transit, I supposed, and it turned out that I was right. New Zero was surging in popularity as a safe city to settle in. I didn't realise it then because I was thinking about tracking down Mercury, but I was seeing the beginning of one of the most important human settlements in that part of the galaxy.

The elevator doors parted, revealing a street level food court. The smells of warm, seasoned foods mingled with a tang that came from self-sterilising surfaces. The sun was down, so there were plenty of customers sitting down to eat, including a group of Issyrians who did their best to look human, but they had the look of a foursome that just came out of the shower with wet hair. If that wasn't enough to signal to everyone that they weren't quite human they were also using broad-mouthed straws to sip from transparent bowls teeming with tiny living fish. Alice never met a mean Issyrian, so I was tempted to introduce myself, but moved on towards the avenue at the far end.

It felt good to be in a place filled with people. The streets teemed with humans in clothing well suited to the tropical weather, short Mergillians in sparse, loose-fitting garments that let their glossy skin breathe, and I even spotted a couple groups of Nafalli. Their long snouts, towering height and long fur were typical of the tree tribes.

Night in Entertainment District Seven was exciting. The last time I'd been through the heavily sponsored city, the streets were empty. Kudzu vines and other aggressive plant life were taking over.

Siren Arms, along with numerous partners, embraced New Zero's ruins. The machines that turned on the people who lived there cleared the corpses away and repaired the buildings as though they had a guilty conscience. In truth, the repair and cleaning droids were just performing their functions. When Siren Arms came along, they only had to stake a claim around their old headquarters, clear away some overgrowth and secure the area.

They built a wall around it using tall metal segments that moved outward as more people moved in. I came in on the side that didn't have them anymore. New Zero was repopulating so quickly that walling the city up didn't make sense anymore. The walls were being recycled into other things, like the road I followed into the District.

Being there, on a street at the base of the new Siren Arms Stadium filled with people, made me feel a little uneasy. I mean, a busy food court was exciting, but it was so packed on the street that I was having trouble getting around. I checked my basic computer for recent events in Entertainment District Seven and saw that a major concert just ended on the nearest side of the massive stadium. Unused to being mentally disconnected from the Stellarnet, I forgot to check on what other shows and matches were happening that night. I looked up the full event schedule for that night.

There were quite a few, but the one that brought that huge crowd onto the street stood out. Mirabel, a human pop star who was already famous on the local Stellarnet, just finished singing in one of the lower levels of the stadium. Dressed in loud colours, imitation high fashion and glowing makeup, her fans were easy to spot. One tall pair of men were in almost nothing at all, but their skin put on a show. Tattooed from their collarbones to their ankles with dynamic ink, Mirabel's image danced on their bodies surrounded by bursts of flower petals and clouds.

They were between me and the nearest entrance to the lower levels of the stadium, where I'd find the first Crush match of the night. "That's from tonight, she was really amazing, right?" said a concertgoer as he pointed at one of the tattooed fan's chests.

"I know, I'm going to add it to my permanent rotation, her style is hotter than a plasma fire," he replied.

I was bumped from behind. A quick check with my hidden sensors told me that it was an honest mistake, there was nothing missing from my jacket pockets and no one tagged me with a tracker or other device. I realised that I was only a few centimetres away from the other tattooed fan then. The playback on his chest was at my eye level. Mirabel doing a quick turn there, her blonde hair transforming into yellow flame. I looked up at him and smiled awkwardly. "Is that a suit, or an active tattoo?" I asked, knowing that it was the latter. I wanted to get him talking, for him to notice me so he wouldn't mind that I was stepping into his space.

"Oh, a full ink nano-spread, honey. I had it done while I was dead to the world," he replied, delighted that I was showing interest.

I stepped around him, pretending that I was giving the work a good look; "That's the way to go, I'm sure. I'd never be brave enough, and I don't think I have the sense of style to show it off. I mean, you'd have to wear nothing at all for your look."

"Oh, when you're this heavenly, you don't want a stitch to get in the way of you and your audience," he stepped back and the crowd gave him just enough space so he could do a turn for me.

I was grateful because it gave me a chance to get almost all the way past him and his companion. "It looks good on you." My voice was unsteady, a sign of the nervousness that was creeping in. I hadn't seen many crowds in The Wastes. In fact, most groups of people out there were dangerous gangs until recently.

Oh, she's nervous. "It's just us super fans out here. Besides, there's nothing wrong with you, cutie, and I love your hair. Natural red curls are so brave right now, everyone's going bald or bold, you know? You doing anything later? Me and my guy are headed to an afterparty. Promise me you'll turn up if I tap you the deets."

I could count the number of compliments I'd received since I was made on one hand, so I was grinning, even a little hesitant to move on. "Uh, sure, maybe. I'm here for Crush though, so..."

"I should have known, with that leather-like art piece you're wearing. Why go to that nasty ruckus when you can party with the sleek and sensational ones?" He struck a pose and ran his hand down the length of his body for emphasis. That wasn't strange to me. Bold, sure, and he was in great shape, so I wasn't objecting, but the dynamic tattoos played a video of Mirabel over his face and everything below that. In it, she was striking a high note, stretching, raising her arms. It made for a completely strange moment, and when I spotted a couple of fans looking at him, their jaws dropped, eyes wide, I grinned at their confused shock. He smiled back at me, probably misinterpreting my amusement, and I looked away, happy that I was about to escape his orbit even though the crowd around us wasn't going anywhere.

Okay, so running around in ruins, talking to strange artificial intelligences, and sifting through old records trying to find out what exactly happened on Tabrus wasn't a group activity. I got to know one person, and he was a complete loner, so my social skills were rusty to say the least. I laughed nervously, realising that I found his invitation more frightening than taking a whole Crush team on alone. Would I go if I didn't have something else to do? Maybe, curiosity can trump anxiety, but who knows? "Sorry, meeting a friend."

He tapped his finger on the back of my hand, right on top of my stamp and the Marble Computing Interactive Stamp glowed for a second, showing that a new contact was added. "Well, now you have to come, you've got all the deets and the drinks are free because you know me. I promise you'll find something there that'll make you forget you're nervous. See ya there."

My details weren't passed back to him, so I didn't have anything to worry about. "Gotta go," I said, laughing, uneasy, continuing on into the crowd. I started to wish I was just there for the nightlife and wondered why Alice didn't socialise much after hours. I remember wondering if that was going to be one of the differences between me and her. Maybe I was going to be more social?

Rain struck the avenue and the hundreds on it through the grate overhead. Some people tried to hide under an awning or in a doorway, so I used the opening to get into the arena. By the time I was through the doors, the rain stopped. New Zero is in a tropical belt, so the weather was often sudden and serious unless the sun was out. As the clouds dissipated, the ghostly blue light bathing the night returned. With two suns and three moons reflecting their light, New Zero was seldom in darkness for more than a few minutes at a time.

Safely through the entrance, I unzipped my jacket, revealing an adaptive top that I'd set to hang loose down the middle. Then I squeezed some of the water out of my hair before pulling it back into a ponytail. There were a few people around who glanced at me, but the five heavily armoured guards inside were watching. I may have looked a little casual, mostly thanks to the top, but I assumed the rest of the look still made them wonder if I wasn't such a casual sports fan. I probably seemed like the kind of person who might be armed, and anyone suspecting that would be right. I wasn't there to see a match. I had other business.

CHAPTER TWO

Ballistic Crush

A guard in heavy-plated armour cocked his head at me as I started for the row of ticket kiosks. The footfalls of his boots were so heavy that I could feel their impacts through the thick soles of my own. I didn't need my scanners to tell me that the armour had strength augmentation technology built in. He was geared up to survive a fight with powerful cyborgs. There were three more like him watching the foyer. "Hey, Red. Let's see under the jacket," he asked in a tone that sounded like he expected me to object.

I knew that was coming. He'd already scanned me but probably wanted to see what his security system warned him about with his own eyes. I pulled my jacket apart and showed off the weapon slung low under my left arm. There were magazines in a holder beneath my right arm. "Violator Seven. It's legal."

"Barely. That's a hell of a hand cannon," he said with an appreciative chuckle. "I'm guessing you know how to use it?"

"You could say that," I replied. Thanks to Alice's memories, I had military training and experience. A little personal experience confirmed that it passed on to me just fine.

"Explosive thermolytic rounds in there?" he asked as his faceplate parted and slid to the sides. He was broad-chinned and clean-shaven.

I nodded. "With an electromagnetic pulse chaser. I'd show you, but I'm late for the match." There was a magazine I didn't want him to see. That one had two normal rounds at the top, but special ones that I designed using Haven Fleet technology. Those were outlawed because they used nanobot technology. I'll explain more about that if it comes up later.

"You're late, all right. The Moles are getting their clocks cleaned, but Ettin is up. No one's seen him play since the League re-formed. I wish I wasn't missing it. Twenty-one minutes left."

I momentarily cringed as I instinctively connected to the Stellarnet and did a search for Ettin. My mind was filled with statistics, highlights from his career and every interview he'd ever given in the space of a second. There was a lot of gore in the playbacks. The guard noticed, and asked; "Hey, you all right?"

"Just remembering the match with Oreole Knights. He trashed Autocrush like he was made of bubblegum and foil."

"Yeah, Ettin has fifteen red cards on record. He'll kill again," the guard replied with a nod and a smile. "You should get in there."

I let my jacket fall back into place, dropped five one hundred platinum coins into a kiosk slot and selected the right event. It spat out a thin plastic ticket that played video directions to the match and I took it from the slot. "Hope you have a quiet night," I said to the guard as I passed.

"Hope so," he replied, re-sealing his helmet. "Pop fans may be a little crazy, but Crush junkies wreck whole city blocks when their team gets trashed too hard—. Just run for the nearest exit if you see something start up, don't want to see you get mashed."

I enjoy passing as a pure human partially because people underestimate me. My skin could trick every scanner I'd found into thinking I was a normal woman in my early twenties. Specially designed layers with refraction and other passive systems that were built in made sure of that. There's also a whole system that simulates bleeding and deeper wounds with optical illusions and holography. It's pretty sophisticated.

Being short helps with the illusion that I'm harmless too. I decided to go low out of convenience at first. It helped me get into tight spaces as I explored and rooted around on planet Tabrus, collecting helpful things here and there. Then I got used to being compact for a human, and it suited the face I liked. If I stood beside Alice, I'd look like her sister with a little less cheek, narrower nose and ever-so-slightly bigger eyes that were green-blue compared to her azure peepers. My hair was longer and wavy, but the same colour.

I made my way down the ramp to Sub level Three, listening to the rising and falling roar of the crowd get closer, louder as I went. A pair of doors wide enough for a hover tank parted and I was in the concourse with the concession area all around me. The booths selling fragrant stir-fries, chicken strips, all kinds of strange things on a stick, candy, drinks and crisps with every flavour of dip imaginable were minded by bored attendants. I hadn't had liquids in nearly a month, and I was running really low, but I passed on that for the time being. I had a Crush player to check on.

Five hundred platinum got me a seat in the front row. It wasn't a premium event and the match was seventy minutes old, so I got in cheap. That seat alone would have been about fifty platinum. The extra four fifty got me a Clubhouse Pass for the night, so I could go down and meet the players. That was the best chance I had at getting face time with Synchron.

I connected to the local wireless network and snagged the maps and other details for the arena. Milliseconds later I converted it into a tactical map and added everything my passive sensors were picking up. The location of everyone in the round arena, the players, and the shapes of every face in the space were loaded in after. There were so many people using active scanners to capture holographic recordings of the game that I could get a perfectly clear image of the space without turning the gain on my own optical receivers up.

I slowed my processing speed back down and disconnected from the network before social media profiles were loaded in for everyone. I could have sorted through all that information in a few seconds, but I really didn't want to. I was only there to make contact with one guy, after all. The junk data from a quarter million social posts wouldn't get a home in my brain, thanks.

My attention moved from the tactical map in my head to the world around me. The tiered seating was filled with people who looked mostly human. Generally, cyborgs have basic, tiny implants that help with medical conditions, correct a sense or two, or provide some minor convenience like regulating hunger so someone can lose or gain weight. The majority of bio-beings don't really want hard tech inside them, that's why brain buds and other computer systems that live outside the skin are still popular.

I found my seat, right next to the aisle. I was standing beside a light cyborg who had a flesh-coloured metal arm, the kind of thing someone got installed to replace a limb lost in an accident. His son, who wasn't a cyborg from what I could see, was to his right. I'd guess he was about thirteen.

A buzzer sounded and the crowd started to quiet down to a rumbling hum. I'd come in at a good time. The players who would be in the final round were testing their cybernetic parts before squaring off. A robot made in the shape of a human with wiry metal arms approached me and I gave him two platinum pips as I grabbed an eighteen-ounce cup. Holding it in front of him, I said; "Pep Slush please." A thick green-blue slush mix flowed from his finger into my cup, filling it in a quick jet, and then he popped a top with a straw onto it.

"Polite to bots, huh? Old school," the man to my right said. "Most people just punch buttons and use as few words as possible."

"I was raised right, and some habits are hard to shake," I replied, taking a sip of the thick drink. The water and high sugar content were good for my liquid reservoir. My systems would sort all that stuff out so it could be used for maintenance, regeneration or fabrication. It was one of my favourite drinks too, thick with a sharp peppermint flavour that was enough to clear my sinuses, not that they needed it.

The rules of the game drifted through my mind as I started drawing on the straw. I won't get into the details, but there's one ball in Ballistic Crush and it's based on the ancient "hot potato" rule. Each team has five players on the field and two in reserve. They can switch at any time and maintenance personnel can repair benched cyborgs while they're on the bench and then substitute them back in. They can't upgrade the players during a match.

At the beginning of each round, the teams face off with a lighter cyborg called the Carrier who stands behind two offensive players and two defensive players. The other team faces off from the other side of the field. The ball is launched from a spinning pillar in the middle of the arena. Whoever makes the catch is protected by their team. Passing is allowed, but that ball will explode like a grenade if it touches the ground. Trying to bounce the ball is not a good idea.

Okay, I started thinking that Ballistic Crush was designed by a sadist when I saw that the goal, a hole only thirty percent bigger than the fifteen-centimetre wide ball, is built into the pillar that launches it. The pitching hole closes the moment the ball comes out. Then the pole starts to lower, eventually revealing the goal, which is at the top. It takes thirty seconds for that little goal hole to be exposed enough for someone to make a shot on it. That means that the teams fight for the ball that whole time. Anyone can score by throwing or stuffing the ball into the hole, but teams get an extra two points if the Carrier does it. That's the lightweight, faster cyborg. Some teams don't even have them. Anyway, if they fail to score after five minutes and thirty seconds, the ball explodes with enough force and shrapnel - yes, shrapnel - to take any player within three metres out completely. Sadistic. Truly sadistic.

I could go on about penalties, white, yellow and red cards along with a bunch of other rules, but I won't. Brain freeze set in. I had pulled half my drink through that straw while I was taking the rules in, looking at the armoured teams setting up in the arena. The kid to my right was staring at me, probably noticing that I started drinking and didn't stop until I flinched. "Too thirsty, brain freeze," I croaked. He and the older guy who was his father according to my air analyser, which caught their

DNA were standing in front of their seats like most of the spectators.

"Hate when that happens," the boy's father said.

I focused on the arena, looking through the thick transparent metal dome at the players. The black and white striped pole was starting to spin. My tactical map marked Synchron and my heart sank. Sure, I cringed at the sensations of human brain freeze, but was able to ignore it an instant later. I was still cringing because I realised that Synchron wasn't just the Carrier, but he was so lightly armoured that his arms and legs looked more like a black and gold skeleton than armoured limbs. His chest armour, or case, as cyborgs called it, wasn't armoured much more, he even had transparent sections that gave the audience a lit view of his enlarged lungs as they inflated and deflated. His helmet looked thin too, I was sure the sleek cyborg would get crushed, or snapped into pieces before the end of the match, especially since his left arm and leg were in pristine condition, suggesting that they were just replaced.

The rest of his teammates dwarfed him, sporting heavy limbs, thick, tall bodies that were a mixture of bare metal cybernetics and armour plates. The other team was set up the same way, "Oh, this is gonna be a massacre," I said as I spotted Ettin, the tallest cyborg on the opposing team. He had Death Labs written down his right leg, showing that he was the only sponsored player on the field.

Oh, Death Labs is an old weapons developer that I thought was defunct until then. I was wrong. Ettin had long arms with long metal branch-like fingers. He flexed them as he leaned forward, waiting for the ball. He was staring at Synchron like there was no one else in the universe, and I imagined that he was grinning behind that face plate.

I wasn't tuned into the announcer's channel, so I almost

jumped in my seat when the buzzer went off. The pitcher pole in the middle spun faster, humming ominously. The board above said the score was twenty-nine to five in favour of the home team, the New Zero Wizards. The holographic display counted down from three, and the ball launched early, on two. I put the nonsensical idea that the counter didn't seem to matter aside as I watched Ettin lurch across the field, breaking into a fast run, his broad metal feet pounding down on the metal floor, past the pole right after Synchron. He was completely ignoring the ball, while his prey didn't seem to care about anything else.

This was it. Synchron was about to get crushed, and he didn't even have the ball. When Ettin was just about to grasp the quick player, extending his long fingers after him, one of Synchron's defensemen collided with the massive cyborg. It was like watching a hover car accident! Pieces of Ettin's armour went flying along with a part of the defence man's fists. Neither of the heavier cyborgs went down as Synchron, undistracted by the collision, deployed wheels from the heels of his feet and started chasing after the Moles' Carrier. The playfield looked large when I sat down, but not so much as I watched him and his team-mates form up and move at incredible speeds in pursuit of the rest of the Moles.

Okay, sure, I'm not much of a sports fan. I've been too distracted, and Alice didn't have much time for that stuff before her memories were copied into my head either. The only time she was interested in sports at all was when it was a part of her course work in the Haven Fleet Apex Officer Program.

I expected a brawl to break out between the teams as the Moles' pair of defence men turned towards their pursuers. Instead, they kept on the move, running and wheeling across the entire field, then around the edge. They were covering for their Carrier, who was leading all but one member of the Moles around. I started to see the wisdom in that. Part of the game is how fast you can move with your team. If you could keep your Carrier and the ball away long enough, they'd have a chance to shoot on the goal.

I thought I was starting to get it when another layer of play surprised me so much that I stood up. Synchron let one of his offensive teammates move in front of him, lean down, and then he sped up and rolled up one of his legs, his back, one arm, launching himself at the Moles' Carrier. He sailed through the air, set to land right on top of his counterpart on the other team and he was bashed away before he touched the ground by a defence man. Synchron flew at least fifteen metres, crashing into the barrier so hard that the transparent metal barrier rattled dangerously.

That was not a penalty. The game didn't stop. Synchron got to his feet, his left arm crushed and twisted, and used the other one to give the crowd a thumbs up as he motored towards his teammates. Ettin lurched after him, but Synchron's teammate, the one already fighting the beast of a cyborg, grabbed him and tried to throw him to the ground.

It gave Synchron a chance to get away and rejoin the rest of his team. Seconds later, they were rushing to intercept the Carrier with the ball along with three of his teammates, and the penalty buzzer went off. The coach for the New Zero Wizards was livid, shouting up at a booth high over the field. "You guys didn't see that shit? Ettin just scrapped him! He picked him up and tore his goddamned leg off then put his head under tread!"

I followed the coach's pointing metal finger and I saw the pile of parts and the bleeding torso of Gyrojim, one of the New Zero Wizards' newest players. Ettin punished him for getting between him and Synchron. "Yellow card! Twenty-minute penalty for holding! Ettin!"

"Holding?" I shouted in disbelief.

Synchron ran over to his side of the arena, where the pit crew replaced his arm and a metal plate on his hip in seconds. The fellow to my left explained the penalty as a medical team rushed out to help and remove Gyrojim. "It's not a red card because Gyro survived. Twenty minutes takes Ettin out for the rest of the game though. They'll have to sub a newbie in and the Moles are closer to forfeiting because they can't field five players."

Ettin took a bow and left the field. The home audience booed with gusto, and I joined in. When I finished, I told him; "It's my first game."

"I can tell, you have that shocked look. It's this one's first live game," he explained, patting his grinning son on the back.

I wasn't having a good time. Maybe if I didn't need Synchron alive I would have enjoyed it, but I knew what it was like to get beaten and blown up. Every time Synchron touched the ball after that I looked up at the counter. I was relieved when they scored, and immediately tense whenever they got possession, which was often. Synchron, despite being a cocky bastard, was pretty good.

In the last minute of the game, the Moles' Carrier had the ball, there was almost no time left before the ball would explode, and the teams came together in a horrific high-speed crush of steel. The Moles' handler got out of there unscathed, and Synchron sped after him while the rest of their teams battered each other in a brawl that had both coaches shouting and holding the tops of their heads.

The game was in the carrier's hands with seven seconds left on the ball. "Don't do it, don't do it," I muttered as I watched Synchron catch up to the other team's Carrier, punch him in the back of the head, shoulder him down and then catch the ball as it was fumbled. That thing was blinking bright red and white. "He did it!" I shouted, tossing the rest of my drink at the play-field. It burst open, spraying green-blue Pep across the glass before it ran down the self-cleaning surface. I calmed down immediately, silently giving myself shit for using a lot more than human strength during my little freakout.

The audience's cheers were so loud that you could feel it in the air. Unimpeded, Synchron pushed off towards the goal in the middle of the arena and threw it right after the ball timer on the holographic board overhead flashed one. The New Zero Wizards didn't need that goal. This was a glory shot that could have killed him. My eye followed the ball, and it exploded halfway through its arc, only nine metres from the cyborg, who stared after it, a grin showing through the transparent lower half of his helmet. "You idiot!" I shouted before the smoke cleared.

The buzzer sounded and security droids rushed the field from all sides to break the brawl up. Two of the Wizards team members were trashed, unable to stand, but three of the Moles' squad were carried off in critical condition. Cybernetic parts were strewn all around the site of the brawl along with small pools of blood here and there. A loud, authoritative voice announced; "Unable to field a full team, the Jungle Moles concede. The match goes to the New Zero Wizards."

The crowd went off again, filling the arena with cheers. Ballistic Crush fans can be crazy. Someone across the aisle to my left brought a Jungle Moles shirt out and the people around him helped rip it to shreds before they turned and shouted; "Syn-chron! Baller baller Synchron!" together, earning a double thumbs up from the player, who was rolling around the arena, raising his arms, directing cheers like an orchestra.

"So, what'd you think?" the guy to my right asked his son.

"Can we come next week?" he asked, thrilled.

"Maybe," his father replied. "Be good and we'll be back."

I stepped out and was about to start for the Wizard's clubhouse entrance when he looked at me. "What did you think?"

I didn't want to spoil their fun, but I was still honest when I replied; "It was exciting."

"You got into it, you'll be back," he said as I slipped away. The seat I'd gotten was perfect, it would have been difficult to get any closer to the doors the Wizards used when they left the field. I walked down into the tunnel and found a few dressed-up men and women along with a bunch of fans who were dressed in old-fashioned jerseys that had foam forms of cybernetic parts built in. It was like looking at a parody of the players rather than appreciation as far as I could see, but I could imagine what seeing devotion like that would be like if I was a player. These people spent hundreds of credits so they could look like one player or another just enough so they could show everyone who their favourite was. I'd be more than touched.

One of them, a fellow with broad shoulders and cybernetic legs that were inexpensive limb replacements, not enhancements, stepped aside to let me into the waiting area in front of the doors and I was gutted when I saw who was standing in a circle of groupies past him. It was Nera, and she hated Alice more than almost anyone in the universe.

Her gaze darkened with recognition. It was obvious in an instant that I hadn't made enough changes to my face to shake a very clear resemblance as she stared. Nera's relaxed chat with the other fans there stopped mid-word and all her attention was focused on me as though she was trying to kill me with her stare or a thought. Then, as though switching modes, she ignored me completely, returning to the conversation I interrupted.

CHAPTER THREE

Alice's Past Collides With My Present

The history behind Nera and her hatred of Alice is pretty simple when you boil it down to bare facts. Nera had a genetic sister named Dela. They were co-captains of a ship that was fabricating highly addictive drugs that they sold along with food, real medicine, and other things they picked up while pirating.

The rest of the Rebel Captains they were with didn't really approve, but they didn't do anything about it until Alice and Noah came along and objected to it. Their ships were much more powerful than Nera and Dela's, and they had connections the Rebel Captains needed, so it was a no-brainer. There were other minor complications, but when it came down to it, Dela tried to shoot Noah, Alice's boyfriend, and he killed her. Nera nearly died too, and their drug lab was destroyed.

Nera's ship wasn't flyable after that and she left to start all over. I have to say, Alice doesn't hate many people. She has a talent for letting the memories of people who screwed her over or outright attacked her fade after they die, and reserves her real ire for people who cause trouble for the masses. Personal hatred isn't something she clings to, and I'm happy I inherited that from her.

Having said that, Nera is a special case. Alice didn't hate her, and neither did I. Pity would best describe how I felt. Bad decisions led to the loss of her sister, her ship, and most of her crew. She also hurt thousands of people, probably killing many of them by peddling narcotics. I couldn't see a situation where I'd want to be in the same room with her and was endlessly suspicious of Nera. The morphing, shifting dress she wore signalled that she found a way to make a lot of money, and she was running with a new crew of well-dressed men and women who hung on her every word. The tickets to get into the Clubhouse were at least five hundred platinum, that's twenty-five hundred credits locally which would cover the rent for a nice place in the city for two months.

One of the super fans turned to me, looked me up and down, and grinned. "Are you some serious secret street metal with hidden augments or something?" he asked.

I looked the term up and saw that it referred to a mercenary with combat-grade cybernetic enhancements. There were covert, or secret cyborgs who hid all their components. "Just a new fan," I replied with a shrug. "Looks like you've been following the sport for a while."

He plucked at his jersey, which didn't have much in the way of foam additions and said "79 HAMMERMAN." It didn't look new but had that look of a worn artefact that was well cared for. "Yeah, I grew up on Tabrus watching the league when they couldn't fill a place like this. I can't believe the league is back, bigger than ever. I'm Orren." I shook his hand and then he turned away from me as the doors opened. A few human-shaped security droids pressed us aside so the two remaining players from the New Zero Wizards could pass without getting tackled by their fans. Some of them were shouting with glee at them as though the players weren't only a couple metres away, while others - like the player who introduced himself to me - offered comments like; 'Good game,' or 'Better than ever.'

A quick lookup on the local matrix for the arena showed that Hammerman was one of the players that was being transported to the Lilac Corporation Medical Centre. He wouldn't be seeing his number one fan that night. I let my sympathy for him fade away as I noticed Nera looking at me. There was a woman in a black and gold suit - the team's colours - close to the doors and Nera was whispering into her ear, pointing in my direction.

I didn't realise that my processing speed was ramping up until I had the urge to draw my weapon and shoot that drug peddler. I forced myself to slow down, calm down, just in time for Nera to come over to me with the suit right behind her. "I haven't seen you here before," Nera said loudly. "So I thought I'd point you to one of the Team Reps. This Is Iyesa, she'll give you a tour of their facility and introduce you to a player or two." At the last instant, she leaned in close, whispering against my ear. "You may have changed your face and slimmed down enough to trick my Bounty Watch program, but I know who you are, bitch. Take the tour and don't come back."

Orren must have had enhanced hearing, because he regarded both of us with a startled look before turning away. One of the guides in black and gold beside the doors to the team's inner sanctum announced; "The players are going to visit the pit for a couple touch-ups and then you can hang out with them for a few minutes. We've got goodie bags and refreshments. The new jerseys are in. They come with a free virtual version, so you're gonna want to grab one of those."

"Hi, I'm Iyesa, I'd love to show you around. What did you think of the game?" the team representative asked as she started leading me through the doors behind the fans.

I was still putting the urge to shoot Nera in the back away as I replied; "It was exciting. I don't know if I can get used to the gore, to be honest."

"Oh, that's mostly for show. There are injuries, sure, but it's almost all minor detachment tearing and impact trauma. As the league grows the teams will be able to afford to buy their players better vital cases and headgear. It'll be bloodless before you know it. What brings you to the game tonight?" Iyesa asked, making an obvious effort to keep things upbeat and positive.

I hesitated on purpose, then replied, doing my best to seem bashful; "I just love the team."

"Is there a specific member?" Iyesa asked so no one else could hear.

Nera and two of her loudly dressed companions disappeared through a side door that closed behind them. I was handed a goodie bag and offered a black and gold jersey. It was for Bioshow, one of the players that was sent to the hospital. This was where I could subtly signal my real interest. "How much for two Synchron extra large jerseys? I'm gonna sleep in them."

The teenage boy who was minding the table smiled and said; "Fifty credits each."

I hated myself a little for playing the fangirl so well, but that faded when I handed the kid twenty platinum and saw the look on Iyesa's face. It was like she'd discovered the lost monuments of Paris, and I'm talking Eiffel Tower here, not some little arch or painting. "Would you like to meet him? I mean, there's a fee, but it's worth it. He's a charmer, and he's single," she whispered the last part, adding; "No strings, no limits."

I resisted the urge to shudder. It wasn't that he was a cyborg, but he was such a showoff and her suggestion at something other than a hug and a holo capture. I managed to fake excitement as I asked; "How much?"

"Well, you can meet him with the other fans. That's part of your VIP package, but it's only a few minutes and you'll be competing for attention. I mean, you can take your chances, maybe he'll notice you and pass you his personal deets, but there's another way."

I knew what she was talking about and blushed furiously. I got that from Alice too, it's not all upside. I wasn't faking. I put the jerseys in my goodie bag and whispered; "It's discreet?"

"We guarantee that the transaction is processed through a secure link that doesn't indicate what it's for. We use it for special collectable merchandise."

"You get a commission, right? I want to make sure you're rewarded for bringing me this opportunity," I told her.

"Of course, my gratuity is built in. It's seventy thousand credits. I realise that's a lot, but we have financing," she replied.

Another shudder moment. I connected to Fi-Bank, put in a credit application for a loan of one hundred thousand credits with the discreet bank, got approved, and nodded. I made sure I'd pay it back as soon as I could get to one of my platinum caches because Fi-Bank's interest rate is literally illegal on civilised worlds. All of them. "If anyone finds out I'll bury the entire league," I told her, staring right into her eyes. "You don't want to know my friends."

The glee fell away from her expression. I didn't know it then, but when I let my processors run all out, which I was doing then because I was getting paranoid. I didn't want anyone to know that I met with him privately because I was trying to make sure that no one could find out that I had questions for him, especially Nera. "I'll make sure he doesn't refuse. Would you like to continue the tour, or..."

"You said he has a suite?" This was my opportunity to avoid Nera and get a private audience with Synchron at the same time.

"I can take you there as soon as you..." she started to say as she sent me the account number for their Special Merchandise store.

I paid her seventy thousand credits milliseconds after it came with a thought. "You have it." I said flatly as I struggled to turn my processing speed down so I could be less... scary.

"There it is," she laughed uncomfortably.

Without another word, she led me to a door beside the trophy case - which was mostly empty - and down a narrow hallway. There was an octagonal room at the end of it, and she showed me through one of the eight doors. "This is his room. You can scan for recorders, but you won't find any. There are refreshments," she gestured to the left where there was a glass door leading to a walk-in fridge that was decked out like a small convenience store. "You'll find this is very comfortable. Please don't touch his civilian body while he's not operating it. Other than that, you have the run of the place until you're satisfied with your experience or for the next eight hours." She recited that as though it was the hundredth time.

I looked around at the room in the half-light, taking in the array of white and gold furniture, a small bar, and a large matching bed. I wasn't myself yet, but I wasn't completely behaving like an old robot with basic programming. "I'll be fine, thank you."

Then, timidly, Iyesa asked; "Are you with Nera's people? Wait, forget I said anything, it's not my..."

"Nera's people?" I asked, raising an eyebrow. "Tell me."

"So... no," she said quietly. "I don't want to know why you're here. If it's for fun, if you're into cyborgs, that's none of my business, but you're not from a rival Org, are you?"

"Like Lost Star?" it was a tag I'd seen more over the last few months in the wastes. An Organisation that was just as much a street gang as it was a crooked corporation.

"Holy shit, I'm sorry, I don't want to get into this..." she started for the door and I got in her way.

"We're just talking," I said, forcing myself to come back down to a processor speed that allowed me to be myself for the most part. "What's Nera doing?"

"Drugs, brain buds with stimulation programs, representing some Org. I don't know which one, to be honest. I stay out of the way. I filter my incoming data, you know? It's breaking the team though, and I'm afraid we're owned by a bad Org."

I stared at her like I already knew. She was so desperate to find a solution to the team's situation that she was willing to reach out to a stranger. "You're just innocent in all this, but you're still happy to collect a commission and turn a blind eye," I told her. I didn't want to let her off the hook completely.

Terrifying her didn't make me feel better. I thought it would have, but seeing her stare back at me looking like she was about to die only brought a wave of guilt. "You're New Zero Law? One of those new street metal bounty hunters? Did he do something we haven't heard about yet? Or, wait, are you here for Nera?" She asked the question so quietly that I needed enhanced hearing to make it all out.

I didn't answer. Instead I stared at her and waited.

Iyesa straightened her jacket and cleared her throat, looking away. "I'm sorry, my curiosity gets me in trouble. Forget I asked, please. I'll make sure Synchron knows he has a guest waiting."

"It's forgotten. Make sure Synchron doesn't draw more attention than normal. I'm just a normal fan who wants some one-on-one time," I told her as she opened the door.

"Just... if I can ask a real question?" she asked, closing the door again but not turning around.

"I'll answer if I can," I replied.

"Are you here for Nera, or do you need something from Synchron?"

Iyesa concluded that I was law enforcement. I was certain of it. "I'm just passing through."

"Damn. I hoped you were here for Nera and her people. You should look into them," Iyesa said before opening the door and leaving quickly.

I waited thirty-three minutes and nine seconds. All the while I sat on the edge of a large reinforced armchair, trying to balance my processing speed so I could still feel a range of emotions while thinking faster than the average human. I considered what I'd learned at the same time.

If I was going on what I knew, it seemed that a criminal organisation might own the New Zero Wizards. It fit. Drugs, an unfair amount of control over the players, violence, spectacle and who knew what else were all signs that crime or crooked corporations were involved. The question was, what would I do about it? Anything? It would be a good idea for me to get away from Nera until I made a decision. That meant getting what I needed there and moving on to my next lead.

"Hey, hey!" Synchron said as he came in. "I hear there's a special fan somewhere in here!"

I put the nearly empty glass of Black Sheep Rum down beside the bottle. I'd drunk a couple of glasses because the real alcohol and other ingredients in the rare drink would be good for my internal systems. I also love vanilla, and I'd never had high alcohol content vanilla spiced rum before. It wasn't something most people drank, and that one in particular was expensive. "Sorry, I had three glasses," I said, dropping a platinum fifty onto the table. The heavy rectangular coin hit with a heavy clank. I had no idea that each glass cost about ten times that much until later.

His fake revelry faded as he looked at the coin, the bottle and then me. "Oh, uh, as long as you're okay. That's forty-three percent alcohol."

"I'm fine. Come on in, take a load off," I said, gesturing to his own sofa. I was back. I felt like myself again, and my scanners picked up nothing abnormal. There really weren't any recorders.

I'd interrupted his flow. The routine he presented to visitors who paid for a private audience was failing. "So, Iyesa said you seem new to the game? You rich and curious, or riding the excitement of your first games?" He struck a pose, and flexed his arms, desperately trying to get back into a role.

"I have a question," I said. "Just a question."

"Oh. So..." he said, surprised.

"You'll have most of the night off," I told him, getting up and going to the bar. "Can I pour you something? I know it's your bar, but I'm guessing you usually do the serving."

"No, but I'm gonna change into my casual bod, all right?" he asked.

"Nope. That's not happening," I replied firmly, stunning him. I was guessing that most of his paying visitors were into that, but I wanted to make it crystal clear that I wasn't one of them. I also didn't want him out of my sight.

He stood by the door, watching me as I stopped midway to his small bar, turning towards him. "I just want to get comfortable. This rig is all about efficiency and speed. It's not made for sitting around."

"It can wait. I'd like to know where I can find Mercury. That's it. That'll earn you the night off and whatever your cut is of the seventy thousand I just paid."

His expression darkened as he answered with a question. "Why?"

"I just need to know." There was no way I was telling him the real reason.

"Mercury is a real danger to my life and wellness, you know? A member of the ninety-eight percent, the last time I saw him. Can't say I know where he is," he replied.

"Ninety-eight percent?" I asked.

"One of those cyborgs that replaced all but two percent of themselves with gear. All he's got is the grey matter he could save. Like I said, I have no idea where he went. That thug totally left us in the lurch. We had to find a new offensive lead, and we've gone through three already. All of 'em had the fear in them. You know, that stupid instinct that makes them forget that they're covered in sport level armoured plates just as we need 'em to charge hard. They hesitate, and someone else on the team gets slammed to scrap. Mercury knew what he was doing. No hesitation when he charged, not ever."

"Where did you last see him?" I pressed.

"You hunting him? Which corp or gov bounty are you chasing him on? I can get you paid off. A refund on that seventy thou for a start, and I'll even leave some of my blood on something for you. Make something in that bag a real collectable."

"I'm not the first to come after him?" I asked.

"Hell no," Synchron replied. "He made a hundred times his weight in plat and disappeared so cleanly that there's nothing to track, not even smoke. Legend like that makes people excited. They want him to do what he did for himself for them. Wait, is that why you're here? You're some heiress who wants to multiply their money? Or do you need something broken into? If you need street metal, then you're in the right neighbourhood, I hear he was a beast when he was an enforcer for hire. He moved on when he got paid for Crush before the Fall though, so that's all ancient history. I mean, if you want brains, he's not the guy either. I don't know how he pulled the max-profit online move that made him mega-wealthy, but no one can convince me that he did it on his own. He was never rich in the brains department. "

"You're spiralling. Stop." I couldn't sound more serious and he did, giving me a chance to ask my question in a different way. "I've got a good friend with an artificial intelligence running in a chip that's supposed to help his brain do things it couldn't before, like recall long-term memories."

"I've heard of that before. This Rafe guy closer to Sol..."

"Yeah, like that," I had no idea what he was talking about, but I was pretty sure I'd turned him in the right direction.

"So, this is about fixing a complicated head injury?" he asked, relieved.

"Exactly. Whenever the limiters on my friend's processor get disabled, it's like he disappears and the AI takes over. It's not a good AI, either," I explained as I watched him move to an armchair.

He dropped onto it. "You don't know what a relief that is. Wow, I really thought you were going to blast my bits off with the hand cannon you're hiding under your jacket. That thing's a nightmare to cyborgs, you know right?"

"I've heard. So, can you tell me where Mercury is, or how he fixed himself?" I asked.

"No, I really can't. The last messages from him sound totally different, like the blending made him like some kinda logic lover with a bad sense of humour. Not totally different from the Mercury I knew, but not the same, you know?"

"Sure. So he didn't leave any trace, not even..." I started.

"It doesn't matter," Synchron said with a shrug, still in good humour. "Not to you. Mercury was a dumbass. In the lower thirty percent of thinkers if you know what I mean. He had no idea how to blend AI with his grey matter. A tech called Bergio told him that it was a good idea after he was so badly bashed in the arena that he was a drooling half-brain, so he did it. Bergio made it all happen. He's an old-school cyber-doc from before the Basic, you know, before The Fall."

"Do you know where he is?" I asked, not daring to look him up on the Stellarnet or any local matrix. I didn't want anyone seeing who I was going to track next and if Bergio was a genius level tech, he definitely had programs watching for anyone who came looking for him.

"Yeah, sure, he's in Errade, up north. He's the only one I trust for Vital Case upgrades. No one else gets that close to my organs," he explained, sliding his hands over the transparent sections as his lungs did their thing.

I'm not squeamish, but it wasn't something I wanted to see. "Tap his deets for me? I can't look him up from here."

"Smart, the arena's network has every kind of snoop prog running, capturing all the activity. Here's the details with no strings. Just tell him I sent you so I get a discount on my next visit, right?" he said, touching his fingertip to the stamp computer on the back of my hand.

Just like that, I had the coordinates for Bergio along with a referral code that would tell him where I got his information. I wouldn't use the code though. Most of them reported back to whoever made it when they got used. It took a little effort to play it cool, mind you. I felt like I was a lot closer to a solution. "Does he do programming?"

"Oh yeah. Whatever you want, everyone who knows about him trusts him, it's been that way for a decade, probably more. I mean, he made Mercury, right? He's a team secret, so don't pass his name around unless it's to serious metal. We don't want anyone to know where we get the code that runs our bods."

"So, he does illegal mods? Works with AI? My friend's problem doesn't involve legal tech," I asked carefully.

"Why do you think he's on another continent? He doesn't want big Orgs to stop him," Synchron replied. "If you've got a couple thousand plat he'll do whatever, especially if you have the parts. I mean, I've only heard of your buddy's problem a couple times, but it sounds like he'd have you fixed up in a few minutes."

"All right, enjoy your paid night off," I said, starting for the door. "I was never here."

"Are you sure you don't want to hang out? I mean, my other body is a lot more casual..." he started, getting to his feet.

"No thanks. I've gotta follow this trail," I replied, tapping the door controls.

There were three heavy combat droids on the other side with suppression rifles pointed right at me. Even with android reflexes, I only had time to curl into a ball before they fired a wave of thick metal mesh at me. The electric charge that followed burned the back of my hands, my face and started working its way through my hair. I ignored the pain. It didn't do much to the systems hiding beneath the flesh, but I let the simulation make my body twitch the instant before the mesh hardened. A normal human would be fully disabled with some pretty serious cuts and burns. They'd still be able to breathe through the tiny gaps in the metal that was shrinking around me, growing more dense every second.

It was the kind of suppression system made to contain androids and cyborgs with real power. I didn't know if I could rip my way out, but I was pretty certain that my artificial flesh would be shredded by the end even though it was much tougher than the real thing. I would be exposed for what I was, and I wasn't ready for anyone to find out. My mind was running full speed, thinking my way through the problem when I heard Nera's voice. "Did you get your money's worth?"

CHAPTER FOUR

A Bad Chair

When your day takes you to a situation where all you can think is; *I should have seen that coming*, over and over again, you know it's a bad one. I wasn't myself as they lowered me into an oblong box that looked a lot like a coffin. I was held stiff from head to toe by a thick, fifty-kilogram coating made from plastics and alloys that didn't let me move a finger. I had room to breathe through tiny voids in the weave. There was a centimetre around my chest and middle that allowed me to pretend to inhale, but everything else was snug and unyielding, even to me.

Nera's taunting sounded like it was pre-recorded, and it was running at a twentieth the normal speed. "You know, I thought you'd have other people here in the stadium. Where's your boy? Your dangerous daddy? We couldn't find any of your friends or your family. My network says there hasn't been any sign of anyone from Haven in the solar system for days."

It was infuriating. Not only what she was saying, but that it felt like it was taking hours for her to finish her sentences while my processor was running hard. I spoke at her rate, trying to move my jaw enough but emitting a muffled; "You want plat? I have piles." My words were muffled because my jaw was trapped mostly closed. I wasn't actually going to pay her off, either. I just wanted her attention so she would use the disperser tool on the cocoon. Just getting my head free might have given me enough room to move so I could break loose, anything would be an improvement.

"Oh, we're past bribery. See ya soon," she said, spraying gas into the box that smelled like feet and sour apple air freshener gone wrong. As they closed the lid, my simulation software analysed it and told me that a normal human would pass out. I let it happen. I don't sleep much. I only nap a couple of hours at a time every few days. I don't think I need it, but I always feel better after, like it clears my head.

I pretended to be unconscious. I was really conserving energy and using passive sensors to explore the tiny space I was in. They'd tossed the goodie bag and my jerseys into the box with me. I don't know why, Nera's a psychopath, who knows why she does anything? The box was transmission-shielded, so I couldn't contact anyone or sense what was happening outside with most of my senses. Cranking the gain on my audio systems, I could hear Synchron. "Iyesa said she could be law. I don't want to be anywhere near a dead cop, or hunter, or whatever the fu..."

"She's not law, you moron," Nera scoffed. "She's on the run. I don't know why, she's practically a princess where she comes from. Her family are famous freedom pricks who got rich when the Carthan Empire handed them a solar system that was too much trouble to leave twisting free. Now they're solar system barons who pretend they founded a democracy."

"So... what? You're going to ransom her?" Synchron asked. "I get a cut."

"You get to shut up, catch the ball and look pretty, you little wind-up bitch," Nera shot back before I heard the door close.

The robots started walking. I started tracking how far and in what direction I was being moved. Bipedal droids have that problem - regular footsteps and easy to detect turning. Most of my sensors couldn't see through the sides of the box, but accelerometers and gyros only needed motion to tell me something.

If I was about to be ransomed, then Nera would call all kinds of trouble down on herself. Alice's family really was powerful, and they had a thick justice streak. I'm not saying that's bad, just that they would be so pissed off that Jake, Alice's Dad, might go on a revenge trip.

The latest news on Jacob Valent was saying that he wasn't a part of the military organisation he helped create. They'd kicked him out, labelled him a war criminal after he plead no contest. He'd taken his old ship back, an updated Earth Carrier called the Triton. If it was true that he'd formed his own private legion, then he couldn't be more dangerous.

If there was someone who could save my butt, it was him or any of his friends. The problem with that is I didn't want to see him or any member of my, I mean, Alice's family. I'm a copy of her, or at least, that's how I started. I don't have a right to call on her family.

I don't feel like a copy. I don't think we even speak or think the same way anymore. In the nearly fourteen weeks since I last saw Alice, I've lived the equivalent of forty, maybe more. That's what happens when you take a complete human personality with all its memories, plant it into the head of an android capable of running it like a program, and then run that personality at high speed for long periods of time. I think differently. Experience has already taught me a few lessons that Alice hasn't learned yet too. I would love to meet her face to face some time to see how we get along, if we could get along at all. I also feared that. What if she was disappointed in me? What if she activated my shutdown code? I was even more reluctant about meeting her people.

Alice's family are good people. That makes turning away from them worse, and ignoring the calls I've gotten from Alice, Jake, and even Ayan - her mother - painful. I needed to make my own life, especially since I always felt wrong in the head. Nothing felt right while my personality was turning on and off. It was like sitting in a chair that was almost comfortable and not being able to leave. After a while, the discomfort is all you can think about, all you can feel. I guess that was the real reason why I was looking for a good programmer who could figure me out and write a patch.

Back to the point. I was stuck in that box, tracking footsteps, listening for anything that would tell me where I was being taken or what would happen when we got there. All the while I was dreading the idea of Alice's family coming to the rescue. I had to get out of the box on my own, or at least be ready when they opened it. There was one good thing about running without any emotion other than anger. Focus.

Sensors collected the little information they could and analysed it. The trickle was maddening. I was used to having all the normal senses and several more exposed enough so I could feel the world around me. It also felt like time was moving along at a half-crawl.

The box was my new home for what felt like a year. Long

enough to get used to it, but I was still furious. There was clarity in the white-hot mode. Then, after my sensors told me that the box was upright, the bottom leaning against a wall so I was face-up, the top opened. I could see temperature outlines through the mesh using infrared. There were two androids, a woman and two men. "She's definitely armed," said one of the humans after he waved something, probably a hand scanner, in my direction.

"I know, our scanners picked that Violator up when she walked into the arena," Nera said. She approached, brandishing something and I was hopeful as I realised that it was a disperser. "I think I'll have that."

"That's a pirate's gun. Made for busting 'bots and weak hulls," said one of her henchmen.

"It's even better against cyborgs," Nera said as she carefully split the alloy mesh right above my underarm.

I calculated how fast I could get free as the split slowly grew. She was slow, taking great care to make sure that I didn't get enough room to move. She probably suspected that she had the real Alice, who always wore a thin under suit that had armour and strength enhancement built in. That sucked for me because it made Nera cautious. "I'm not Alice."

"You know, so many people say; 'don't judge people on appearance alone,' but I just can't shake this feeling. I can see that you've changed your face just enough to have a resemblance, measure a centimetre shorter, slimmed down and even remixed your DNA. Yeah, we did a deep scan. It still doesn't change my gut feeling. You're Alice."

"You're crazy. I'm not her. You do not want to know who I am." I was warning her. I remember the millisecond decision that was made then - that it would be the last mercy I would offer.

"I think I have to. You even sound like her. There are people here who will be really excited at the opportunity to figure out how you changed your DNA without really messing yourself up. We could market that process, and I'd catch a royalty."

"Corporate? You've gone corporate?" I asked, irritated at having my jaw trapped.

"Not quite. Well, I guess so, but explaining it to you would be a waste of time," she said as she reached through the slit she'd made in the thick mesh holding me still and started pulling my jacket aside. "The corp is in the expansion phase. I signed up when this crew was just a wasteland salvage crew with a territorial streak. It's a transformation I can take some credit for, but you seem to know all about change."

She pulled my Violator Seven free from its holster and found my Passport Chip. She took that too. "Don't take those."

She brandished the handgun appreciatively. "Spectral Dynamics has stopped selling these to the public. They're a bitch to get your hands on, so, thanks. It is a really ugly weapon, but I think I'm warming to it."

The passport was real. The government on Tabrus formed a little while ago and I applied for local ID as soon as I found out. They were hungry for money, so they were giving them to anyone who would step into a scan booth and pay twenty-five hundred platinum. It's a lot cheaper now, but the wait is longer and I don't want to get into a real scan booth. Hacking the last one took three tries and nearly a week just so I could be sure that it couldn't see through my fake humanity. I still don't know if the high-powered deep scanners can defeat my skin and see the metal beneath, but getting caught would draw the attention of every law enforcement agency and bounty hunter in the solar system. Androids aren't allowed to pretend to be human here.

I know, it may be hard to believe, but losing the gun was worse. It was a gift from Alice. Strange, but it felt like I was getting her blessing when she took it from her bag and put it in my hands. "Let me out. I'll join you."

"Did you seriously just offer to join me? Your boyfriend killed my sister. I saw how you were with him, the breakup must have been murder. Where is he? Maybe I'll consider dropping you off on Theta if you tell me where I can find him. I'm sure you can find a gig there as a miner, or as a doll for one of the ore barons."

Theta, a world that didn't have a proper name, was a hot rock with half an atmosphere, a bad radiation baseline and tens of thousands of mines. The miners weren't hit hard by the Fourth Fall, when emotion-enabled artificial intelligences went berserk on humans, but the corporations and law enforcement that ran the world were. The miners reorganised into their own gangs and companies. It wasn't a place most people wanted to hang out. I'd be fine, but getting off that world might be a pain in the ass.

I was already planning payback as I watched her check the safety on my weapon and nod with satisfaction. "Not talking. We have a drug that'll change that. One more chance: where is Carnie?"

"Try the Rose System," I replied. That was mostly true. I suspected that he was in the Rose System with Samurai Squadron, but couldn't say for sure. I don't think I'd be doing Nera any favours if I sent her in that direction, though. Samurai Squadron, the Triton, and everyone around Carnie were geared up for war. I didn't think the Darmen would have a chance in a confrontation.

"Picking the one place I'd rather leave behind, not smart, little chickie," she said, tapping my forehead with the muzzle of my own gun.

I wanted Nera for myself, that's why I started struggling when she turned away. The mesh wouldn't give. I had a couple of non-lethal restraint weapons stashed away, and I was starting to reconsider carrying one as the stuff didn't even crack while I momentarily put all my strength into one good push. The skin under my arm split, and I stopped. If I was in some kind of stronghold, people would be monitoring the room, and I didn't want to show anyone that I was an android.

"I'm being called away by less personal business, but I'll be back with an injector and more questions," Nera said, carrying my weapon and my passport with her. She'd forgotten to take my stamp computer. There were security droids in the room. These things would come together, but I was still trapped. Even if I could make all the computerised things in the room work for me, I would still be doing it from a vulnerable position, and the Violator could do real damage, even take me out. "Here, get her out of that cocoon, put wrist restraints on her. She doesn't leave this cell, do you understand?"

"Yes, Ma'am. The security..."

"The droids will guard the door when you're done and she's in nothing but cuffs, and I mean nothing. Scan her once you've got her down to her skin. Her people have serious tech in their clothes. Oh, and don't get distracted. Alice has a way of tricking people into thinking they're her friends. Don't listen to her." Nera spoke to them like they were slow teenagers, and they didn't look happy about it, but listened to every word.

The security androids, which were nothing special, just human-shaped robots that were low-end military models without built-in weaponry, settled in at my right and left. One of her underlings started dissolving the cocoon. It seemed to take forever, especially since he started with my middle and worked his way down.

I need you to understand something. When my processor is cranked up high, and it feels like the world is running slowly, I'm not myself. Nothing looks or feels like full-speed fury. My instincts are different when I'm running high speed, and I wanted out. I wanted to catch up to Nera.

Patience doesn't last when you're consciously experiencing your world one millisecond at a time, and I'd reached the end of mine. When the guy with the slicked hair finished dissolving the mesh to my ankles and started working his way back up, I created a full network connection to my stamp computer.

It was one of the better models out there, but it would still slow my online speed down drastically, so I started queueing commands slowly. Well, slowly for me, but I connected to the guest account that the building created and looked through their company directory.

Nera had done well for herself, rising to the level of Public Relations manager. I chuckled at that, and the slick-haired guy who was working on dissolving my cocoon looked up. "Tickles," I told him.

"Just don't do anything when I get you out of there. I looked you up, you can't surprise me," he said, shaking the disperser wand at me.

I wanted him to get back to work. Most incapacitation webs didn't take that long to break up, but they were taking their time, probably to make sure that they didn't burn me. While that was nice, it wasn't necessary. "Sure."

"I'm serious, if you make a move, do anything I don't like, I'll turn this all the way up so you come out without skin," he said menacingly, poking my stomach with that thing.

"I won't," I wasn't lying, technically. "You know they make dispersers that break this up in a few seconds, right?"

"You got one in your pocket?" he asked.

"No," I replied.

"Then shut up." He was focusing on my stomach as the metal webbing retreated, revealing bare skin.

While he was distracted, I used their guest wireless network to look everyone in their Leadership Directory up. I was downloading every social media and public-facing fact they had out there in a few seconds. It took longer for the information to arrive than it took for me to ingest it. I was searching for a security gap, and I found one.

Tony Rapson was one of three Communications Managers. That was a bullshit position. He was a thug who was locked up right before the Fourth Fall hit in Stonehold Prison. When the therapy robots got infected by the Holocaust Virus and took the prison over, he was waiting to go into storage. Under normal conditions, he would be hooked up to a full-dive system so he could serve his sentence in a virtual world while machines took care of his body.

After they were infected, the therapist bots were anything but normal. They decided that the fastest way to kill the majority of the humans in the place was to flood it, and they did. Thanks to a couple of lucky shorts, doors were left open, and Tony Rapson was able to swim free. He joined the Darmen gang shortly after and they started pillaging the mostly empty world of Tabrus after the robots calmed down. I sped through video and holographic playbacks in my head, ignoring the long list of offences he committed during the first few months after The Fall. He was a murdering slaver, a thug, like I said, but he adopted a stray dog who he called Bugs. I turned my attention back to the local network and started considering what his password may be.

I had his parents' names and pictures of how he was with them. Since he seemed to like his father more, I took that into consideration. There was a pattern of numbers in his speech. I could tell he was a legendary bullshitter from the candid record-ings I had, which numbered in the thousands and found the digits he used most when he was lying. I analysed his speech, his body language in and out of a business suit, and saw that he was actually a fearful person. If he wasn't following hedonism or greed, he was insulating himself against future wrongs and harms. Nothing else seemed to matter to him. That was his life, those were his tendencies. I chose him because he was easy to read, there was so much footage of him committing crimes that wasn't deleted yet. After what I saw, I thought he deserved to get into trouble.

Based on that, and a list of his most commonly used expres-sions, I created a short list of passwords. I tested those on sites that he visited outside of the company, you know, entertainment aggregation companies that streamed music and oil wrestling along with a few long-distance communication applications. After nine tries I found a password that he used on seventeen different sites, and then I tried two variations on the Darmen Corporation's digital security login.

It worked. He had lower administration privileges, which was good, but not good enough. After checking through five hundred thirty-one communications that he'd had with members of the company after they started changing from a gang to a corporation, I discovered that, true to his fearful idiot nature, he'd bribed a tech to give him one of the top security passwords for the company. It took me a few seconds to review twenty-six hours of footage to find an angle where I could see him looking the password up on a Flexi smart paper tablet.

I waited for the system to catch up with me, and detect that I was an intruder for a few seconds. Their security software wasn't slow, it just didn't notice that Rapson wasn't in the building but he was logged in locally. They'd either under-spent on it, or they weren't smart enough to use good programming. They probably trusted manpower, that people could keep their building and other concerns safe. Their stupidity worked for me.

I used the security password to drag all the information I wanted about the building into my head and then to connect to one of the androids in the room. To my surprise, it worked. I was seeing myself through the sensors of one, then both of the androids. Giving the software that governed them orders seemed easy. As a test, I had them switch places. They did so, crossing the room and taking positions opposite each other. They didn't even raise suspicion with the humans in the room, which was weird. Most people, especially criminals, were watchful when it came to machines with the most basic artificial intelligences.

I looked up my position in the building and found that I was on Subfloor Three, beneath the storage level. Nera was almost on the roof. There was a shuttle waiting there. I wouldn't get to her in time, especially if I wanted to hide the fact that I was an android. "So, we get the rest of her stuff, right?" the one named Stan asked.

"I guess so. Nera already took a couple things, so we get pickers' rights," the one named Burke said. "We have to check her for anything that could be trouble anyway, right?" Burke looked me up and down then got back to work with the disperser. I'd seen both their records. He was the one who joined the company right before it started to go corporate.

"We've got to get her stamp off, at least. That's gonna hurt, it looks weave-bonded," said Stan. He was listed as a janitor with the company, and started six days ago.

They both spoke as though I wasn't there. As though I was completely powerless, and I was eager to prove them wrong before I left.

Burke finished dissolving the mesh holding my face and started to work down from my left shoulder. At my urging, one of the androids stepped forward and gently took the wand from Burke and said; "The prisoner has been classified as dangerous. We will complete this task."

I made the other android say; "Your supervision is not necessary."

"I'll tell you what's necessary, bot!" shouted Stan.

Here was a hothead who thought subjugating robots was some kind of revenge against whatever he'd seen other machines do to him or his people during The Fall. It wasn't a rational way of thinking. There was no emotional programming in that bot, so it didn't care, and punishing one bot for something another did to you wouldn't fix anything. I directed Sec-Droid Thirty-One to turn the disperser up so it would sting, but not burn my skin. Instead of breaking the cocoon down half a centimetre per second, it was turning it into liquid at ten times the rate. My whole head was exposed shortly after, but my hair was still trapped, woven in. I had the android move on to more important areas, like the remaining weave holding my arms.

When I opened my eyes and looked into Burke's, I said; "You should go." I spoke quickly, but not faster than a human was capable of.

"What was that?" Stan asked.

I started feeding the security system a fictional playback that I created myself. One that showed that everything was normal, I was being uncased by the android while the humans stood around. At the same time, I replied to Stan slowly, over-enunciating my words; "I said; you should go. I'm a dangerous captive."

They laughed, and Burke presented a pair of cuffs with a thick line holding them together. "It'll be fine, sweetie."

I operated the android that wasn't freeing me directly. It took the handcuffs, grabbed Burke and cuffed him.

Stan drew his handgun, a shined-up thing with big shells. He fired without hesitation, putting a neat hole in the android's head. He managed to destroy one of its motion sensors, which didn't stop it as it grabbed the weapon with one hand, and his throat with the other. Stan tried to squeeze the trigger, but the android's fingertip was wedged behind it, something I'd made it do intentionally.

The android's other hand squeezed around Stan's neck, crushing cartilage, bone and flesh together. He dropped to the floor as though he was a puppet with his strings suddenly cut. Burke stepped back; "Holy shit!"

Androids on my level were on their way, altered by the gunshot and I reached out to them. At my prompting, they stopped and waited for further instructions. "You should have listened to me, Burke," I said through clenched teeth. I reached further, to the shuttle that was lifting off from the roof.

The security system aboard was separate, so I settled for the next best thing, taking control of the anti-air gun installations around the top of the building. They turned, aimed and fired, rattling a short barrage of rounds at the shuttle. It had energy shields, so it survived the first volley. The second ripped into the passenger cabin. I was aiming for Nera. It was an emotional decision. I should have taken its thrusters or power plant out. The pilot let the shuttle fall past the edge of the building and out of half the anti-air battery's firing arcs. It didn't matter, the shuttle was safe the next instant as anti-intrusion software finally kicked in, blocking my access to the turrets on the roof and inside the building. I was relieved to see that the safeguards only reacted to the turret controls.

I called my motorcycle and gave it a route to get to the

Darmen Building, then unlocked the storage room I'd left it in. It could move through every fast lane in the road system because it was unoccupied, so it would be waiting behind the building in seven minutes and twenty-eight seconds. "She didn't say you were with a hacker group!" Burke said as he backed into the corner.

"Any gang or corp who can't handle a hacker isn't worth its space on the Stellarnet," I replied as the android finished freeing my boots. I let the hair that was stuck in the weave fall away as I stepped out of the box. There was no need to rip or force it free, I was able to release as much or as little as I liked, and I was left with a curly bob cut. "Do you want to die today?"

The sounds of gunfire and shouting outside were starting as I ordered every android to attack everyone with a weapon. The ones in my room turned towards Burke, who had a pulse pistol on his hip. "Just go, I won't stop you," he said, struggling with the cuffs.

"This building is home to a bullshit outfit of serial murderers and slavers. I'm going to end it. You're all just cruel bags of meat to me." I told you I sounded different when my CPU cluster is running hot and I'm pissed off. "Give me your weapon."

I'd seen thousands of hours of footage from the Darmen while I was digging for details on Tony Rapson. If there was a real government on Tabrus, most of the members would have been executed or imprisoned, but the planetary government was a joke. Their police force only protected the politicians. The New Zero cops were so over extended that they didn't have time to investigate companies like Darmen, let alone take them out.

On the brighter side, there were Bounty Boards, but I hadn't bothered signing up as a hunter. I hadn't considered becoming part of the law enforcement ecosystem, and I was sure it would take a long time for hunters to get around to the Darmen gang. I wanted them to suffer for what they'd done as a gang and for being associated with Nera, so it was up to me.

As Burke carefully took his weapon from its holster I calculated many different ways to end his life. At a glance, I saw holographic evidence of him killing three people, one of them a young teenage boy, and I suspected that I'd find more if I kept looking.

I didn't feel that I was the one to dispense justice, but I had a high appreciation for it. When I was running high, people who killed innocents were disposable at best, and targets if I had time. He tried to turn the gun on me at the last moment and I forgot myself, grabbing it at full speed.

I was lucky that the security system wasn't recording what was really happening in that room, but a fiction I was making in my head. I looked into his eyes. They were deep brown, open wide. "You didn't have to kill that family for their hover truck."

"How could you know?" he asked with a quivering chin.

"It'll be fine, sweetie," I told him as I turned away and ordered the androids to relieve him of his eyes and his skin.

No one got in my way as I strode through the halls, up the stairs and through the rear exit. Androids, cleaning bots and every system I could access were working on killing everyone who carried a weapon. As a corporation filled with former gangsters, that was the majority. I was surprised at how bad they were at defending themselves.

I only had to wait ten point five seconds for my bike to arrive, and I rode away, sending the command to delete all records of what happened, and then report the company as fraudulent to every other corporation on the planet. With the near absence of law in the solar system, that was the only way to make sure that everyone there would think twice before working with them. I also made sure that people would see the most violent crimes committed by everyone associated with the company whenever they looked them up on the Tabrus Local Matrix. I could have done most of the last part with practically no hacking.

My processor started to slow down as I rode through New Zero. By the time I was on the outskirts of the city, I felt like myself again, and it wasn't good. Guilt and despair at how I'd treated everyone in that building, the absolute violent gore of it all, overwhelmed me. I nearly crashed as I got off the raised freeway.

I needed physical relief, and that meant whatever was left in my stomach was coming up. I could ignore the impulse, and disconnect my emotions from my body, but that would have made things worse in the long run. Rum and Pep made for a bad mix on their return trip as I left it on the side of the road and retched for a while for good measure as high-fidelity memories of the carnage I'd caused played back. Sure, there were a lot of bad people in that building. The corporation was crooked, but I could have gotten out of there without killing anyone.

Even better, I could have moderated the violence so only the people who got in my way were harmed, and only as much as was necessary. Some of the employees who were killed weren't murderers or former gangsters, but they were armed, and I decided they should be attacked for that reason alone. Again, I'd taken things too far. I'd been cruel.

I turned my processing speed up a little, just enough to take the edge off of my personality, numb some of the more punishing emotions and let my physical simulation work. To anyone passing by, I looked like someone catching my breath on the side of the road. That's how I felt, too. The human simulation is a good thing. When the body feels better, the soul - or personality in my case - does too. Well, most of the time.

Before long I was back on my bike, racing towards my biggest stash site in Hibora. What I'd done would draw a lot of attention, and if Nera survived, she'd try to get whatever was left of Darmen to come after me. There was a good chance that I would face more trouble soon thanks to my overkill urges.

CHAPTER FIVE

The Hibora Cache

Tabrus is big for a habitable planet, almost point one percent larger than old Earth. There are several major corporations trying to take developed territory. Siren Arms was the first of them, and they even registered their claims with the Tabrus Republic, the planetary government. Like I said before, they have barely any power but were happy to legitimize all of Siren Arm's claims for a three percent export and sales tax.

Since almost no one respects the Tabrus Republic, and claimants are responsible for policing their territories, other companies and gangs are always testing the least protected borders. They make claims of their own with statements on the Stellarnet or Local Matrix that invite customers in and warn everyone else to stay away. So far, less than ten percent of the planet's land masses are claimed, and most of those claims are illegitimate.

The reason why I'm going on about this is because the cache I was going to in Hibora was fully legitimate. I actually bought the land from the government under the name of Rogue Vagus. Hibora was a unique spot, surrounded by Tabrus Quartz quarries. I owned one I liked and used it as a landing pit. There were ramps cut into the walls broad enough for tracked haulers that were three stories tall so I always felt like I was in a land carved out by giants when I rode down to my ship. Most of the quartz was white, and the quarry was far from exhausted. It reminded me of snow, which I hadn't seen with my own eyes yet, but there was something simple and magical about the spot. It was also huge, with a storage cave that I kept some of the machinery that worked here before.

The ship, called the Uwebo, was a medium-range passenger transport that I found in perfect condition. The sad part? Its owner was dead. Killed the moment the Holocaust Virus that infected every artificial intelligence on the planet that was programmed with emotions turned. The ship sealed up while Banna was having a party on the ground and the artificial intelligence stopped re-oxygenating the air. They suffocated. I found it months later. The corpses had been taken away when the droids were cleaning up the planet.

Banna had no will on file and no relations who would come for the ship, so I claimed it, the government accepted that, and I used the platinum I found aboard to pay the salvage tax. My timing was dead on with the quarry and the ship. Corporations were about to move in to mass-claim huge portions of the planet for almost nothing, paying the government for the land and everything on it.

Siren Arms was bidding for an entire continent, the largest on the globe, and it looked like they'd get it according to Hart News. There were just a few details to hammer out, probably how much money they'd have to pay the Tabrus Government, if they'd provide defence services for the rest of the planet, and whether or not Siren would become another government. I was hoping they would, because the records I could find during late night browsing sessions suggested that no one went hungry or homeless in their larger colonies.

My Quarry Cache would be in their territory, and I'd probably get to keep it, but I'd pay taxes to Siren Arms. I hoped they wouldn't be high.

As for the Uwebo, my backup ship, I wiped all the data drives, including the artificial intelligence and made the ship, which wasn't really my style to be honest, my own. It was my backup until I sent the Envoy, a ship I stole, away as a decoy. It was also where a few people knew where to find me.

I carefully manoeuvred my bike up the ramp leading into the Uwebo's hold. It was a small cargo space that I'd crammed full of supplies, including a reserve of platinum coins that filled two square one-metre crates. You're probably thinking that I'm rich at this point, which isn't too far from the truth. I'd been running around in the wastes for months, making platinum a high priority. Cash is king, as they say, and platinum is cash.

I tuned my internal scanners to detect it and amplified that using a device that fit on my head. I looked for ships, equipment, high-density data drives, and all kinds of other valuables including rare gemstones that could set me up. I found a lot, building caches across the continent. One of them was blown out by Citadel and the Order of Eden. The most valuable stuff, a message meant for Alice along with some extra data, got to the right place. If you know the details, you're aware that I pretended to be off-world when she was here. I still regret that.

The lights in the cargo hold were already on, and there were bootprints matching Lat, one of the few friends I'd made. I lowered my hover bike onto its stand and he met me at the door.

Lat was tall with a powerful build. I liked his broad shoulders but wouldn't tell him. It didn't take much social stuff to confuse him. He was a framework, a flesh and blood soldier who was manufactured by the Order of Eden using a system of fabricators, energy converters and generators that were built into his artificial bones. There could be tens of thousands or more men out there who looked exactly the same. He was the first one I'd met who escaped the Order and wasn't re-fabricated back to his default state so he wouldn't remember anything.

Wearing a device on his head that was a lot like the one I used in the Wastes to enhance my scanning range, holding an extra large spring roll, he regarded me with surprise. "I almost took off. You didn't respond to my transmission."

"Sorry, I shut my receiver off and..." I looked down at my stamp computer, pulling my glove down enough to see it. It was blinking, I had three messages. "...sorry. Is everything okay?"

He looked at me like a guilty puppy. How can someone over two metres tall look so innocent? "I passed through a Siren Security Checkpoint by mistake. They..."

"...saw your framework systems and tried to arrest you as an Order operative. Where was this?"

"Rinnel. They were having a fair, you know, with costume people and rides?" he asked, unsure if I'd ever heard of such a thing. "I thought I was going around it, but there was this place with holographic monsters, and I got turned around."

"A haunted house," I said, nodding. I'd seen a couple in a very old period movie from the Remmybase, a massive, curated collection of ancient movies, videos, music and other kinds of entertainment from Pre-Second Fall Earth. "How hard was it to get away? Did anyone get hurt?" Asking the question seemed hypocritical after where I'd been, what I'd done.

"A broken arm, maybe, I had to push one of the guards away. I lost one of your shuttles too. A cargo lander. I was there to trade five hundred litres of processed regeneration gel," he explained, trying to throw in details that were probably meant to soften all the misdeeds he thought he'd piled up. "I did what you said; made sure that no one was watching my salvage operation, took only the most valuable stuff, and traded it over a thousand kilometres away, at a smaller settlement that might need it. I had the money when things got complicated, and I made sure I didn't really hurt anyone more than I think I had to. Rogue, I know I said I didn't need your help anymore when I left, but I saw things out there. You warned me, and I didn't listen. I thought I could handle the wastes, but I went without food for days at one point, nearly got killed in the end. I got the transport you gave me back though, and then I came on this good find. I thought everything was fine, I even got paid. I was eating cake on a stick when... the holograms were so weird, all skeletons and weird things, and I ran for just a second. That's when I passed through the scan gate and there were alarms..."

"It's okay, it's okay," I said, taking his free hand and looking up into his eyes. "You made sure you weren't followed?"

He nodded. "No one's been within ten kilometres of the pit for two days. I've had a lot of time to figure out where I went wrong. I get it now, I wasn't ready to go. I don't know what I need to, I've been studying like you said. I hope it's okay that I'm back, I was afraid you wouldn't be here."

I had nothing but sympathy for him, so saying 'I told you so,' didn't even occur to me. It would have been better if I tagged him, checked on Lat to make sure he didn't get into trouble. "So, people chased you before you got to the fair?"

"Yeah, that was a few days after I left. They stole the transport while I was defecating behind a tree. Then they came back and chased me around for a few days. I got the upper hand on one of them at night. Don't worry, he's alive. I stunned them, tied them up and took all my stuff back. I was hundreds of kilometres away when they came to. That's when I started thinking I left too soon. I'm sorry. You were right," he finished, finally starting to calm down. It wasn't like him to get worked up. Lat is the quiet type, it took a lot to make all that talk bubble to the surface.

"Okay," I said as made sure the ramp was closed behind me and led the way into the main cabin. There was a table, seating for four that included a soft corner sofa, and several food fabricators built into the wall with a sink and cupboards. "How did things go in Rinnel before you got spooked?" I wanted to get him talking about something positive, a success. It sounded like he'd already learned his lesson from the other stuff.

"Well, the Public Exchange was happy to see me when I showed them a load of unexpired recovery gel. I had a pocket full of platinum. I wanted to explore. There was so much I'd never seen before because of the fair, but they also had a weapons restriction, so most of the perimeter was being scanned. I got around that, but ran into it when the monsters started chasing me. I didn't know they were holograms. That won't happen again," he spoke in a rush. "Are there a lot of fairs?"

"No, it's the first one I've heard of since The Fall. Maybe a few travelling ones are starting back up. Don't worry, I know you'll be more careful." Then I had to remind him of something that I knew he didn't want to hear. "If you take the pill I made for you..."

"I know, I'd go to sleep, the framework will replace itself with real human parts, and I wouldn't have to deal with this. I still have it." he held the little box hanging on a chain out for me to see. "I just don't know. It feels wrong."

"It sounds too much like dying, I get it," I replied, sitting at a table littered with containers marked as Oriental Delight. I turned one, looking at the ingredient list for a container that once held egg rolls. "These aren't good for you. Too many chemicals and they use old stasis fluids in the sauce to keep it all edible for decades."

"I know, but it's so good," he said, finishing his oversized spring roll. Then he spoke around it as best as he could. "So, I can come back? I can watch your back next time you go out."

"You can stay," I replied. "The scavenging and salvaging thing isn't going to last much longer here though. I'm going to have to find real work eventually." I looked at the Flexi page he had on the table. It was propped up against an empty package of noodles. "What have you been watching?"

"Don't worry, I was using your spoofer. No one knows anyone's here." That wasn't an answer, and he was avoiding my gaze.

"What's up?" I asked, resisting the urge to link to the tablet. "Don't worry if you think it's embarrassing, I've seen it all..." I was reaching for it.

"It's news. Ayan Anderson's shuttle was shot down by Citadel terrorists. She's fine now, though. Gone into hiding, so she's safe," he explained.

I found myself wishing that he was watching anything else as I picked the tablet up and viewed the Hart News recap of events surrounding her. Ayan was Alice's mother, and I still felt like she was mine too. She was also the new founder of the Haven Solar System, the place all of Alice's relations called home. A place that still felt like home to me.

Citadel, a powerful ally to the Order of Eden, hid a ship in the smoky atmosphere of a planet in that system, and they had just shot down Ayan's shuttle. Laura, her adopted infant daughter, was aboard at the time. I was thankful that my body could cry, because it felt like a year's worth of fear and wrath was shed with every one of those tears as I watched the rest of the report.

The Citadel ship had been destroyed. Their leaders took credit. Laura's baby carrier had sealed in time, protecting the infant, so she was unscathed. The report didn't go into detail about Ayan's injuries, but she'd been found, treated in the hospital, and was already in hiding. As the summarized report came to a close, Lat said; "I'm sorry I let you see that. I know you don't look at them. You connected me to their job training system, and I follow the Royal Family. I'm sorry, I didn't know you'd be back and I forgot to turn that off."

I wiped the tears away and nodded, relieved that Ayan and Laura were safe. I hoped to find anyone and anything from Citadel on Tabrus or the Order of Eden so I could hunt them down. The only reason why I didn't go after them when they last visited the planet was because I wasn't ready to see Alice yet, and I regretted it deeply. "It's okay. They're alive. They're okay. If they're hiding, well..."

"If they can hide as well as you can, they're safe." He wanted to reassure me, but I think my tears freaked him out. "Do you know them? They look like you, a lot, I mean..."

Turning my processor speed up wouldn't help. I was already pissed off, so I just had to deal with it. A long inhale and exhale got me a long way. "What matters is that they'll be safe. They've got resources you couldn't imagine. It's not your fault that I found out. Well, it kind of is. You left this thing on, but news would have gotten to me somehow, and like you said; there are a lot of messages."

"So, you do know them?" he asked. A lot of people looked to

the Haven System, saw Ayan as some sort of queen, and acted like they were seeing a new Camelot or something. I wasn't surprised that he felt the same way. His thinking was generally simple because he was still learning about, well, everything other than how to be a soldier. That's why I had him working his way through Haven's education system before he got impatient and left.

I got up and went to the small bridge to check the ship's communications system. It was one of my data caches, securely collecting whatever was sent my way through the communications node in orbit that allowed for near-instant interplanetary networking. It was designed by Haven, and put there by Jacob Valent, Alice's father. There were dozens of messages from Alice's family, and half a dozen from Alice herself. Even Ashley Lamport, someone Alice always liked but didn't know extremely well, had sent a few messages. I didn't know she was aware that I existed.

Lat followed me and looked over my shoulder. He didn't know better. Privacy was a concept that he didn't understand.

I wanted to watch the videos, read the texts people sent me, even call them back more than I could say. There was a problem though. As I looked through the names of the people who were trying to reach out to me, I could perfectly recall their faces, the way they spoke, and even feel what it was like to be embraced by Noah Lucas, Alice's boyfriend. He still felt like mine. These people still felt like my people, and my processor cluster ramped up. It was instinct, my emotions and personality faded, became secondary, and then inactive. "You really know them," Lat said, glancing at the screen and then at me.

My face must have been statue still, except for my mouth. "I need the ship. You can only stay aboard if you listen to me. First order: stop eating that crap. There's nutritious food base in the dispenser."

"Yes, Ma'am," he replied quietly.

Moving to the pilot's seat, I rapidly changed the permissions in the system so he had full access to the ship systems. I wasn't worried about him betraying me, Lat hated the Order to his core. His entire batch came out of their boxes wrong. They found the murders the Order committed in the Iyagda System horrifying. He was the only one who got away. The rest were regenerated. I met him when I borrowed the cargo ship he stowed away in. He was terrified and starving. He may have had a rebellious streak, but I was starting to believe that he needed to follow someone more. "You have access to everything on the ship. I'm taking off in thirty seconds."

He paused for a moment, staring at me, and then nodded. "Where are we going?"

"To see someone who might be able to help me with a problem. Strap in." I said as I scanned for intruders, found none, and then started the launch sequence. I made sure the Pit's security systems were active and plotted a course for the coordinates I'd gotten from Synchron.

CHAPTER SIX

Bergio

A Stellarnet search on Bergio gave me access to a wealth of information, but it was all old. He was a cyberneticist with a heart of gold. A war-zone chop doc in his youth, which was over a century ago, and he'd saved thousands of soldiers. He could do with scrap metal and old batteries what some labs couldn't accomplish with the latest technology.

Since then he opened a practice on Tabrus, performed installations for free to the poor, and started offering regenerative treatments a couple of decades ago. Not all of his patients had limbs and organs replaced with metal and plastic. He was a programmer as well, on the cutting edge of digital biological bridging technology like cooperative cognition. He helped a lot of people who could barely think due to degenerative diseases or brain damage get their lives back.

Then the Holocaust Virus came to Tabrus and machines

piloted by artificial intelligences with emotions in their programming turned on everyone. His trail ended there, but the Pro-Bio Movement, which was against all artificial intelligence, listed all of his research as detrimental to humanity and other biological sentient beings. They were also the ones who named the new era following the Fourth Fall, the Basic Era. I wish that name wasn't sticking, but it was. It still irks me that people call the new age we're in 'The Basic,' I don't really know why.

I shook my head as Errade's skyline came into view. Unlike New Zero, it was a mess. Pristine buildings were mixed with others that looked like they were about to fall over. I could even see one in the distance that was burning like a massive torch from the middle up. No sign of fire response anywhere. The perimeter was well armed with big disintegration cannons on towers, though. Even if half of them were offline, it wasn't good to break the rules within the expansive city. Just one could ruin my day in a second. Navnet knew where I was going, I'd registered a flight plan.

The cannons swivelled slowly, ready to defend the city. They were mostly pointed up. Assaults from above were more dangerous than my flimsy little ship, especially since gangs and corporations were warring over the city block by block. Orbital strikes weren't unheard of.

I opened a channel to Local Navnet Control "This is The Uwebo, Shuttle Class, TR-Five Zero Zero Two Nine Five. Requesting perimeter clearance. I have a plan on file."

"You are clear. I'm being paid to inform you that Vongo Limited is offering a twenty-five percent discount for full protection," came the response.

I tapped the payment into the communications panel built into the flight system. It was a legitimate company that paid out, according to their reputation. They would make sure nothing fired on my ship while it was in the city limits, and give me the value I claimed if they failed. I insured my ship for three million credits, about what it and the contents were worth and paid them twelve thousand up front. I was using money from that loan I took out earlier, but kinda hoped that someone got a shot off on my ship while we were away. It was a nasty way to turn it and all the cargo into Tabrus Credits, but, hey, they offered.

"Welcome to the Inner City. You're on your own if you go street side," the tower said as the transaction cleared.

"We have insurance for ten hours," I said as I put the ship down on a platform that hung off one side of the middle of a building. There was one on each side, balancing things out, but I had to wonder if the structure was sound as I heard some unwelcome creaking. I noticed that my forward landing gear needed servicing too. The pneumatics weren't holding pressure the way they should.

"Will they pay us if the ship falls off the side of the building?" Lat asked as I locked the controls.

"No," I replied, getting up and going to the cargo bay at the back. He was right behind me. I pointed at the weapons locker. "Sidearm and armour."

He pulled the top of his Order of Eden armour on without questioning or hesitating. The alloy plates were once green, but he'd repainted them dark blue.

He'd only seen my softer side, but I was keeping my processors running higher than usual, so that wasn't what he was getting at the moment. I had issues to unpack. You know, big emotional questions and one of the worst things I've felt so far - longing for relationships that had to end because they don't belong to me. There would be a time to face all that, but it wasn't there or then. "Listen, if this goes well, I'm going to say a lot of things that don't make sense at first. I'll answer all your questions later."

"Like why we can't both be in the bathroom at the same time?" he asked.

"No. That's different," if I were feeling more like myself I would be amused.

"It doesn't make sense though. You were in the shower, and I had to use the toilet. There was a divider, so nothing would have splashed either way..."

"Lat. Focus. If something goes wrong, we get out as fast as we can. I'm going in for help with my head. Something is wrong with me, and I've hurt people. I can change sometimes, and not in a good way. That has to stop." I didn't believe it as I said it, but I knew it was my mission. I was extremely good at following a directive when the processor cores were hot.

He nodded at me, and even though his gaze couldn't be more serious, I was sure he didn't fully understand everything I said. That was enough for me though. I strapped a Rexo Revolver to my thigh after checking the ammunition. There were two shells with the same stuff that trapped me and three more with a softer plastic capture mesh loaded. After moving a few crates aside, I pointed to a half-metre cubed, secure box. "Carry that for me?"

Lat dutifully picked it up and regarded me with wide eyes when he heard the jingle of loose platinum coins. "This is heavy. Is it all..."

"It's all plat. It'll probably be what this costs," I said with a nod. The ramp at the rear lowered. The wind whipped the platform, its high humidity making everything feel thick and heavy.

We got as far as the door and the crackling of a speaker overhead drew our attention. "If it isn't the hacker of the day. Why are you and an Order of Eden Framework Soldier darkening my door?"

It was Bergio, I recognised his voice from the few interviews he'd given over the years. "I regret what happened at Darmen Corporate Headquarters. I'm looking for help. I don't want it to happen again."

"You're human. I just triple scanned you. I don't have the tech to declaw you unless you want me to install something to slow you down. You can go to any street chopper for that. Maybe therapy is the answer? There are two practices in the building. They should be open in an hour or two."

"C'mon, let them in. We never get visitors anymore," said a high, creaky voice.

"No, you never get visitors. I don't want visitors," he replied. Then he turned his attention to me. "Listen, you seem like a perfectly normal lady. Well, physically. Whatever you want me to install won't help as long as you're hanging out with a gang of hackers willing to reenact their own version of the Holocaust Virus in corporate gangland. You should take that drone standing behind you and leave town. Get off the planet. Switch ships somewhere and drop off the Stellarnet so your hacker friends can't find you."

He assumed that I was with a whole gang of hackers because I'd turned automation against my captors earlier that day. "I was alone. I didn't need anyone's help. The logs to prove it are in my head. If I can trust you, then I'll let you see for yourself."

"Unlikely. I don't do bio-brain dumps anymore either so..."

I was in full calculation mode and if there's anything my logical persona doesn't like, it's facing barriers. That's the only way I can explain what happened next. Something from early memory resurfaced, and I believed it would convince him. I leaned forward and whispered; "I have a secret to tell, and I'm leaving out the whistles and bells." I sent the address a message with records from my earliest transformation from software to human and waited. "Also, I have all this money."

Lat shook the crate, making platinum coins jingle. "It's heavy."

"Aw, let them in. You like money and other people's problems," the smaller voice said.

The doors opened and we passed inside. "What does that mean?" Lat asked. "Whistles and bells?"

I didn't answer him. We walked into a neat, clean apartment living room. A small cat greeted us, saying; "Hi. I'm Mimi. Take your boots off." She sat and watched us, her tail twitching.

"I'm Lat," he said following instructions as he stared. "You're a Kawaii Kitten?"

"I'm an enhanced, unique, purely biological, adorable miniature cat of carefully curated breeding. Bergio said you're a soldier who wandered off his battlefield. Is that true? It might not be true. He can be wrong about things." She cocked her head at him, staring.

"He's right, I did leave my battlefield. I ran though, so he's a little wrong," Lat replied.

I finished taking my boots off and straightened. "Where is he?"

Mimi regarded me with narrowed eyes. "You look wrong somehow. It's like there's nothing happening on your face. Is it switched off? No happy or sad?"

"Yes," I replied. To this day I wish my other side had met Mimi first because it would have been a lot more fun with a full spectrum of emotions.

"Huh, I didn't know humans could do that. He's had weirder

things visit, so whatever," Mimi said, turning and leading us through the living room.

We went down a hallway then, and, knowing that I'd have to reveal that I was an android anyway if I was going to trust this guy, I scanned through every door on our way to its end. There was a dining room, kitchen and an empty waiting room on one side. To my right was a fabrication room with metal granule storage, a bio-grow room with a pair of eyes and a hand under construction as well as a store room with well-organised stacks of cybernetic parts. That last room was the only place where I found combat-grade hardware. Oh, all those doors were closed by the way. I was snooping, but for a good cause. I didn't want to get jumped.

The metal doors at the end of the hallway parted and the cat walked straight into the laboratory. To the left was a self-sterilising operating area with high-end surgical arms hanging from the ceiling, and his office was to the right. Holograms and wall displays scrolled with code from the Holocaust Virus as well as the viral cure for it. The words I spoke into the speaker, originally from an ancient song that confused many and enlightened a lucky few, were highlighted in several sections of it. "We're stepping on a trap," I told Lat. "Don't panic."

As we crossed the threshold bands lashed out from the floor, capturing our feet and legs up to the knees. They also wrapped around our sidearms. Lat struggled, dropping the box of platinum coins. It made a huge racket and the lid broke open, spilling a few coins out onto the white tile floor.

Bergio ignored it, turning and regarding me. He was wearing a hooded sweater that was missing its right sleeve. I guessed that was intentional because his right arm was a bare metal cybernetic limb with tools built into the forearm and hand. His left eye was cybernetic, much like the one Alice had for a while. Other than that he had a blonde-white beard and a full head of hair to match. "Okay, I hope you're not just spouting something you read on a hacker forum, because I'd like to know more. Those words only repeat in one song and a notorious virus-antivirus combination. A virus I cured when it hit Tabrus before the anti-viral transmission arrived."

"You cured the Holocaust Virus here?" I asked.

"Well I got help from a wandering AI, but he's gone so the credit is mine. No one will listen to me though, so it's not worth much," he explained.

"Wait, let me guess. The Iron Mind?"

"How do you even know that name?" he asked, surprised, probably amused, spinning his chair and slapping his slippered feet in time to stop when he was facing me. "And what was that other data string you sent me at the door? Consciousness transfer? It looked like it was made for an old Vindyne operating system."

"That was me. Well, not all of me, but a snapshot from the moment that I became human the first time. I used a Vindyne lab experiment to transfer myself into a human body," I explained, leaving Alice out of it. Sorry, I didn't want things to get even more complicated, sister.

"Wait. The Order was invented by people who worked for Vindyne before they were bought by Regent Galactic. They included those words in the virus in an attempt to frame Jonas Valent for its creation," he said, bringing up a documentary on Freeground and the Order of Eden along with a number of other historical pages. He was surrounded by holographic data in moments.

"I hate it when you get all excited and play with your

computers really fast. It's just too much talking and lights all at once," Mimi said as she stretched out on a blanket bunched in the corner. "I'mma nap now."

I was amused at how she didn't care about what was going on, even though there were strangers in a tense situation. Then I realised that my processor cores were slowing down. I was becoming more myself. It was a relief and a weight. "The Order included some of my code in the virus. I had become human in the meantime. The data to prove it was there. Something's happened since, and I've changed. Again."

He waved his bare metal cybernetic arm through the air, moving holograms around. "I'm catching up. The connections are there, but you're not Alice. She's alive. She's been here on Tabrus, there's footage. You're similar, but…"

"You could call me her sister," I said, feeling even more trepidation about revealing that I was an android, but I was standing there - whether I liked it or not - and I could not find any legitimate dirt on Bergio. "An advanced android."

He stepped through the wall of holographic text then and looked me in the eye. His mechanical gaze scanned me over and over again, the irises opening and closing. "You're not, there's no seam, I'm seeing normal tissue and organs and normal human function…"

"It's a trick. I can show you," I said, dreading what would have to come next.

"Well, if it won't do harm, then please do," he said impatiently, still smart enough to stay out of arm's reach. "I've made full bio-shells, but there's always a seam somewhere. I'd love to see craftsmanship better than mine. Then again, if you're just a disturbed human who thinks she's an android, I'm going to have to charge you for whatever medical services you incur during this demonstration."

"Don't worry." I looked to Lat first and said; "Don't freak out, all right?"

He was as stiff as a board, staring, wide-eyed. There wasn't much I could do there. He'd either freak out or not. He couldn't run off since his legs were still trapped.

I turned all my attention to Bergio. "This is no fun for me, and I need you to keep my secret." I formulated a simple escape plan, just in case he didn't. It wouldn't just get me off the planet, but the solar system.

"Okay, okay, show me," Bergio said, watching.

"Did someone say secret?" Mimi asked lazily as she rolled onto her back and looked at us.

I gave my armoured skin layer and the flesh beneath it the instructions necessary to make a split from the neck up that would allow me to pull the two halves aside. I did so and revealed my entire android head. There was no bleeding because my skin can come off like a floppy suit if I tell it to. I don't like to do it, especially when I can see myself. I knew I was revealing a mechanical skull with eyes and teeth that were still perfectly human looking. Mimi had the biggest reaction, shrieking; "Put it back on! Put it back!" before scurrying under her blanket.

"Hush, it's perfectly fine," Bergio said over his shoulder before taking a closer look at me. "You're a combat android. That armour, it's made of a new, advanced alloy. We don't even have a name for it. I need higher resolution scans."

I sealed back up and shook my head. "Nope. It's proprietary. Not my secret to share."

Mimi slipped out from under her blanket and ran over. "Do it again!"

"Sorry, show's over," I told her, surprised.

"No, really, do it again. I didn't get a good look," she said, tapping my foot.

"Weren't you about to take a nap?" Bergio suggested by way of asking.

"Treat?" she asked.

"Nap."

"Fine," she sulked, slowly returning to her old blanket. "Then treat."

"Okay, so that was very real," Bergio chuckled. "Wait, why don't you go back to your people to fix..."

"...a programming issue. I think. It's complicated."

"I might be able to help. But what's the reason you're coming to someone you don't know instead of your designers or maintenance people?"

"That's what's complicated," I said. "I'd rather fix it on my own, or find help on my own." I looked at Lat then and saw that he was looking down at me uncertainly. "You okay, Big Guy?"

"Sure. You've got silver bits under your skin. I've got silver bits under mine, we're all good. Makes more sense now I guess. No way I'm taking that pill, though."

"Okay, maybe I'll want to hear more about that later," Bergio said as he held a high bandwidth antenna closer to me. "So, let's talk about what I saw you do today. You hacked the Darmen Corporate Headquarters and killed nine people using their own machines because..."

"Nera, one of their corporate officers, captured me, stole my favourite gun and my passport. She had no idea what I was," I replied. "Wait, only nine people died?"

"Right, that's how many it took before they realised that the attack would stop if they put their weapons down. It took longer than you'd think, I don't think they hire the brightest people there, being a former Wasteland gang. I wasn't going to say this, because it's not exactly decent of me, but I don't think it could have happened to a better bunch of people. Now, can you transmit your process? A capture of everything your computer is doing right now."

"Sure," I said.

"Rogue," Lat said, tapping me on the shoulder. "Getting a cramp."

"Can you?" I asked Bergio, glancing down at the bindings.

Distracted by the flow of data he was watching, he pressed two buttons on the wall and the ultra-strong, stiff bands wrapped around our legs retracted back into the floor. I could have pulled free anytime, but that wouldn't have made the right impression. I checked down the front of my face for any lingering seams with my fingers and was satisfied that my skin was resettled. Lat reassured me a little more as he looked at me closely. "Can't tell you just took it off and put it on again. You're good."

"This isn't..." Bergio started as he looked through several streams of scrolling text. "I mean, there are elements of an advanced artificial intelligence reminiscent of a tiny piece of the Holocaust Virus."

"Because they copied a little of the Alice AI code when they made it," I explained again.

"Right, I see that. It's what I'm not seeing that's the problem. Did you send me a whole capture? Is this the whole range of memory addresses?" he asked.

"I sent you a whole second of all the processes I'm running. Here, I'll stream everything passing through volatile memory," I told him, doing exactly that. It was liberating, sharing what was going on in my brain.

He looked at several holographic displays hovering around him and shook his head. "There's less here this time. What's different? What are you doing that you weren't the first time?"

"I'm not processing as much," I replied.

"More. Be more descriptive but general, simple. I need broad sweeps, not technical details," he replied, beckoning with his artificial hand.

"Okay, I'm not thinking as strategically," I said, watching him impatiently gesture for more. "My processor cluster isn't working as hard, so my personality is coming out more."

"Oh, oh, so you can think with nearly pure logic, completely ignore your emotional self?" he asked.

"Well, nearly. My logical side has a temper. It tends to take things too far. That's why I'm here," I explained.

"I have a theory. One moment, I'm investigating," he rapidly typed on an old keyboard for a moment. Several gaps in the code he was reviewing expanded and filled with red text. "This is the kind of thing I should be seeing here, here and here. All the red is stand-in code my programs inserted to represent things that should be happening in your computer right now. Physical control, emotional comprehension, motivations, subconscious interactions, perception interpretation, the kind of thing that a program that thinks its human, or behaves like a human should be doing, but it's just not there. It's just missing. There's only one explanation," he said, getting out of his seat and coming over to me.

We were nose to nose when I asked him; "What?"

"You won't guess?" There was a playful look in his eye. "Come on, you'll get it in three tries or less."

My mouth opened, but I didn't have a response. "I don't know." After another few seconds I ventured a guess by sharing one of my worst fears. "Maybe it's a script my program builds on and alters fast enough to trick me into thinking my softer side is real?"

"Oooh, a genius guess. There are ancient programs that did that before they figured out real emotional coding languages. Wrong, though. Guess again," he said, excited.

Relieved that I was wrong, I tried again. "A safeguard in my system isn't letting me send you everything?"

"One more try," he urged.

"Ooh, I like this game," Mimi said, looking up at me. "Can I have your last guess?"

"Sure, I've got nothin'" I replied.

"She has two brains!" Mimi shouted triumphantly.

Bergio rushed back to his seat and deleted everything but the red text. "Give the prize to the Kawaii Kitten who's supposed to be napping! All this code my system created to stand in for what's missing is happening somewhere other than the computer you think you're using. The reason why one snap-shot is different from another is simple. Sometimes you use one computer more than the other. It's a switching system with shared responsibilities. That's not interesting on its own, however. One computer is protecting the one I can't see, that's what's interesting. "

"That makes a lot of sense. I lose touch with my emotional side... sometimes," I replied. "Can you fix it?"

"Why? Do you feel ill? Mentally, I mean?" he asked.

It took me a moment to find the words. Even when I answered, they didn't feel accurate. "I'm off balance. Nine bodies dropped thanks to that."

"Did you know you had two computer systems in there?" he asked, pointing at my chest.

"I had no idea," I replied, looking down even though what I'd see there wouldn't help.

"Have you scanned yourself?" He picked a high resolution hand scanner up, then put it back down, probably realising that it wouldn't do any good unless I opened my chest up.

"I don't have to. My systems are monitored. I'm just aware..." I trailed off as I gave it a try. I got what I expected. There was no sign of a second computer system. "There's one box behind my breastbone with everything inside."

"Define 'everything.' What's in the box?" he asked.

After trying to scan through it, I shrugged. "My processing and memory systems. I thought that was all I needed to know, I never questioned it. I can't see inside now that I want to."

Bergio got to work, running several searches on the massive chunks of code I sent him and finally snapped his fingers. "Gotcha. I see the problem. I can patch that. Your software has a safeguard that prevents you from using your own sensors to scan there. Just there. I can patch that so you can see what's in there. Nothing else will change. The problem is, you're going to have to stop thinking about it for a while."

"What?" Lat asked.

"How?" was my question.

"You'll have to stop pondering the mysteries of your minds for a bit. Just think about other things for a few minutes or something. Your system is aware that you're trying to puzzle this out and it won't stop running the program protecting the box in your chest until you aren't focusing on it anymore. My patch will take that opportunity to alter the program so you're in control of it, then you can scan as much as you like," he explained. "Almost finished."

"Really? You're quick," I said.

"It's a simple patch if you have my kind of experience. It's specific to the current version of your software, so even if someone else gets it, it'll be useless. They probably won't even know what it's for unless they pick it apart. I also have a few thousand terabytes of custom code from past commissions, so I have a unique head start," Bergio said as he typed up a storm. "I'd be done by now if I didn't like the feeling of a keyboard."

"He likes to brag," Mimi said, rolling her eyes.

"Hey, you guessed right, so you're no mental light weight yourself," I told her.

"Thanks, it's all the brain juice he gives me," she replied, rubbing against my foot.

"Done. Pay me and it's yours. The computer in your chest is more than capable of checking it to make sure there's nothing malicious in there, and that it does what it's supposed to," Bergio said, his cybernetic finger hovering over a worn ENTER key.

"How much?" I asked.

"Whatever's in that crate," he replied.

"Done," I replied, watching him press the key. The little patch, only sixty-four kilobytes, came in through a direct connection then. My computer system went through it line by line and I couldn't find any sign that it would do something that he didn't promise. It wasn't spaghetti code, either, but logical, well annotated, efficient programming. "Nice."

"You checked that in under two seconds? Impressive," Bergio said.

Just to make sure, I checked it again. I wasn't a great programmer, but my mind has military grade defence software installed, and it didn't see any problems. At worst, the patch wouldn't do anything. At best, well, who knew where it could lead. I took a deep breath and ran it. "I don't feel any different."

"Like I said, you have to relax so your software doesn't think it has to defend itself from you. I have a theory about that, if you're interested." He was on the edge of his seat, obviously excited to share.

"There's a good chance you're right, so sure," I invited, bending down and stroking Mimi's soft fur.

"Your makers didn't want you to find out you were an android. Not just that, but they didn't want you to know what exactly you had running inside that little breadbox if you actually did. Maybe because it's just like you said; your parts are proprietary high tech. Maybe it's something else. The answers are in there, or they aren't. It's for you to discover eventually," he said, waving the thought away as he turned his attention to my code. "Come back if something breaks, but it won't be my fault. My patch only opens a door, or a window, or a skylight, or something. What you see is your maker's fault."

"He's going to stare at all that new code for a while," Mimi said as she slowly walked back to her blanket.

"A long while. The low number of errors I'm seeing is incredible. Is this tech on the market? Who makes it?"

"Haven. They have a habit of over-building things," I explained, stopping the stream of data going to his local network.

"Maybe I should go there. I hear good things," he muttered as he scrolled one holographic display then another.

"I'm surprised I didn't figure this out on my own. I used to live in code, move from system to system," I said as I turned the box of credits upright. I was nearly drowned out by the coins inside.

"Wait, wait, wait," Bergio said as he plugged his android arm into his desk. "You don't feel bad, do you?"

"You mean I don't think I should have realised all this earlier? Yeah, I'm feeling like I missed something pretty obvious," I sighed.

"Look at it this way. You were never meant to know anything about your own systems. I bet if I took a tour of all your data, I wouldn't see anything about how you were built or what you were for other than what you discovered during your own experiences. All you knew was that there was something wrong, and you were smart enough to find someone who could help.

Someone who would rather befriend you than betray you. That is smart, and the best you could do under the circumstances."

"She's pretty smart," Lat said out of nowhere.

"Wait, how did you find me again?" he asked.

"Synchron referred me," I replied, watching the expression on his face wilt as I did.

CHAPTER SEVEN

Time To Leave

Bergio was frozen in place for a moment. Everyone, even Mimi, stared at him, and I made the mistake of scanning his body. His heart rate was up at panic levels, respiration was increasing, and fight-or-flight tension was spreading across his entire body as the chemical levels in his blood shifted in the same direction. Even still, his words came with a forced calm. "I'm happy you didn't tell me Synchron sent you at the door, because I would never have let you in."

"He told me you did work on him," I replied, hoping for an explanation for his alarm that wouldn't cut our meeting short.

"Synchron can afford the premium I charge violent androids because he sells everything he has the instant it's in his hand. Whatever he hears, sees, every rumour or little piece of data is assessed by his little mind for its value. Then he trades all of it for influence or credit to whoever will pay.

Whoever you angered, this Nera person, I suppose, has been approached by him and she has probably paid for whatever he could tell her." As he spoke, he moved about the room, picking up a shoulder bag, opening a high cupboard to retrieve a sachet and a few other things that he stuffed in there. "Nera is one of the leaders of that gang of junk-loving, drugged-up losers, and everyone knows she takes her temper out on everyone who goes against her. That's me, because I'm helping you, so nothing I care about is safe." He scooped Mimi up and handed her to me.

I was shocked. So was she, and she clung to my hand, asking. "What's going on?"

"You remember how I told you that someone would come and adopt you someday? Well, she's either going to be the one or she'll find you a forever home, okay? She can protect you."

"But I don't know her," Mimi replied, stretching her paw out towards him.

"I do. I've seen her code. I've seen her recent memories through the data link. You're going to like her more than me, and you'll be safe. That's all that matters now, Mimi. Be a good girl and go. Listen to her, do as she says."

"This is my home," Mimi objected.

He held her chin with his fingers and looked into her eyes. "You're finished, Mimi. I can't make you any more capable than you already are. Now you need someone like her so you can see more, learn more, experience more of what life can offer. Do as Rogue says, no matter what. I've seen her heart and know more about her story than she thinks. You can trust her."

"I don't wanna go, I like it here," Mimi objected weakly.

"I'm finished improving you, so you have to go," Bergio said, walking back to his desk where he reconnected to the terminal.

I was speechless as I carefully held the soft-furred kitten in my hand. She looked up at me, her eyes so sad. "I can really trust you?"

I liked Mimi right away, so I wanted to say 'yes' immediately, but I knew I would be taking another life, one that was more helpless than Lat's, into my hands if I did so. I looked at what Bergio was doing and saw that he was deleting all evidence that I'd ever been there. He was in a hurry, too. "I can stay and protect you, Bergio."

"No. This was going to happen eventually. Using the money that comes from violence to help more innocent people doesn't change the consequences of doing business with those people. I've been making that trade for a long time, well before the Crush League returned. I'll face whatever comes alone, I've gotten out of worse situations, but you have to hurry. They're coming, and I don't want them to use my guests or Mimi as leverage," he replied in a rush.

I connected to the Stellarnet and saw what he was talking about. There were fifteen ships, a few of them fighters, belonging to the Darmen Corporation flying around the city's walls. Another group was on their way. Troop ships with a hundred-ten-metre-long light frigate at their centre. They were moving slowly, signalling the city. Then I saw that someone was trying to trace my connection back to my physical location. The trace came from an Order of Eden Stellarnet address, their Intelligence branch for the Edwyn Cluster. They had been watching for me, tracing for me, and I knew for a fact that they discovered which city I was in before I disconnected.

It would make everything worse if I was found in Bergio's lab. I couldn't even guarantee that changing my face would trick anyone. Then there was the chance that someone would use the tiny cat in my hand for leverage, and I couldn't abide it. "You can trust me to get you to a safe place, Mimi."

A plan was already in mind, but Lat wasn't ready to hear it. "You're going to save her and yourself. Unzip the bag."

He picked up the shoulder bag, did so, and I put Mimi in there with all her things. She fit with room to spare, and I zipped it up most of the way so she could poke her head out. "He's going to take you out of the city to a safe spot."

"But Bergio said I should trust..." Mimi started to complain.

"You can trust me, and I know he'll take care of you while I go another way for a while," I told her.

"Are they coming now?" Lat asked.

"They're all coming now," I told him, going to the credit crate and picking up two handfuls. I put the coins in his hip and back waist pouches. "Take public transit. You're going out of the city. Buy a cheap but reliable hover car and take her to The Bog Box. I'll meet you there when I can."

"Where are you going to go?" he asked.

I was surprised. It was as close to resisting instructions that Lat had ever come, and I was proud of him, but annoyed at the same time. "I'm going to clean up my mess." Then, I made the next part an order. "Go. Wear your mask."

"Yes, Ma'am," he replied, turning on his heel the moment he finished. His strides through the apartment were long and quick.

"They're coming. The main group of ships just got permission to fly into the city," Bergio said from his terminal. "All evidence of you coming here is gone, except for you."

"Thank you, Bergio. I'm sorry for the trouble," I said as I turned to leave.

"I love that cat," he said. "She's not a normal Kawaii Kitty. She's more intelligent, will live much longer and she'll need people, stimulation. You can give her that. Take care of her, and remember; some trouble is worth it."

I nodded at him and then ran through the apartment at full

speed. Lat had taken an elevator down to the lobby. I went in the other direction, to my shuttle. I could hear Bergio moving the box of platinum I'd left behind as the main doors opened. He was most likely hiding it, and I was glad I left it with him. He deserved it as far as I was concerned. Bergio showed me what I needed, and I knew what to do next thanks to that.

The Quarry Pit was publicly registered under my name, as was the Uwebo. That's why I sent Lat off to one of my unregistered caches, the Bog Box. It wasn't as nice as the Quarry Pit, but I'd stashed supplies and equipment there. I momentarily pictured Mimi coming nose to nose with one of the bullfrogs that lived around it and smiled.

That mental image was forgotten as I boarded the Uwebo and got to the controls before the rear ramp had time to close. I took off, rushing the warm-up sequence. The combat computer was slow. I didn't bother upgrading it because I never wanted to take the thing into a fight, but it finished booting up and warned me that five tactical systems were locked onto me. One belonged to City Defence, which was normal. The other four were unknown ships belonging to the Darmen Corporation. Three of them were fighters. The fourth was the light frigate.

Even though my processor speed was ramping up and I was shedding worries about harming civilians, I still didn't want to fight within the city limits. As I flew towards the nearest perimeter wall so I could get out of the most heavily populated area, an argument was going on in my head. Well, it was more of an urgent thought process. It sounded a lot like this:

Nera will never leave me alone. I have to take care of her.

I could escape, leave the solar system.

She will put a Watch and Report Notice on me. I'll have to change my appearance more than once. How will I ever feel like myself if I have a hundred faces?

Identity is internal. The exterior is superficial.

I'll have to leave everything I own behind.

I can always find or earn more stuff. Maybe I should change for a while.

The Order and Nera's paths are converging. What if they become allies? She could become more powerful. That'll be my fault.

The last point stopped the turmoil. Nera was becoming a larger threat to my existence than anything or anyone else. Her hate for me was a benefit, I could use it to lead her away from everything I cared about, even my new acquaintances.

Lat knew how to hide. I made sure of that. There was a filtration mask in his pocket that could cover his entire face and I was certain that he put it on before the elevator got to the lobby. I was also fairly sure he'd protect Mimi, because he'd shown protective instincts with me more times than I cared to count. They had a better chance at escaping and hiding than I did, especially since the Darmen Corporation didn't know about them.

I could improve their chances by making sure Nera caught me, but I didn't have to make it easy for her. The city wall was coming up, and there was a fighter waiting for me right on the other side. I registered a flight plan with Navnet that informed the nearest tower that I planned to leave the city's airspace and travel to Greenfield, one of the star bases in upper orbit.

After getting some altitude, I increased thrust to the maximum the ship could handle in the atmosphere and listened to the hull as it groaned under the pressure. The inertial dampeners whirred loudly as they fought to balance the weight inside the ship and compensate for increased gravitational forces. Navnet informed me that I'd incurred a two thousand credit fine for exceeding the thrust limit near the city, but I knew the worst anyone would suffer if they were standing on top of the buildings behind me was a harmless, short warm gust. I used the computer to pay the fine as I watched the tactical monitor.

Darmen's ships were turning and accelerating after me. The nearest of which was the fighter that was waiting. It opened fire as I passed, missing. It only took about ten seconds before it started to catch up. "I really need my own Clever Dream," I muttered as I set the autopilot and slipped out of the seat.

Back in the small cargo hold, I threw crates aside as I dug for a suit of mechanised armour that had been put into storage mode. It, along with a weapon case, was buried at the back, under my other box of platinum coins and a few flashy weapons that were meant to satisfy looters.

The ones I kept that armour and weapons in, the most useful ones, were in battered containers that were made to look pretty uninviting. I'd even dragged them through a bog a little. The mechanised armour was a full exoskeleton covered with metal plates and fully articulated hands. It was modified and calibrated to my dimensions. I dropped my jacket, converted my blouse into a long-sleeved, high-collared shirt and unclasped my boots.

The emergency audio channel received a transmission from Nera. I could hear her speak through the communications panel in the cockpit. "This will be easier for you if you land. I don't want to shoot you down. That would be messy."

"You don't want a confrontation with me," I told her, my tone utterly emotionless. "I learned how to fight from experience, the military, and Jacob Valent. If you come for me, I'll punish you."

"Big words from a little girl who strayed far from her friends and family. Land and I promise you'll survive what I have planned for you," she replied.

I stepped into the armour. It activated, rising up to close around my body. It wasn't anywhere near as good as what Haven Fleet used. The plating did have some stopping power though, and the strength multiplication systems gave me the freedom I needed to use the full capacity of my android frame. I was many times stronger than the suit, but anyone looking at footage of me throwing hover cars around while I wore it would assume that it was the exoskeleton doing the work. The helmet closed around my head and I picked up a pair of military-grade sidearms. One was a pulse gun that connected to the suit's power pack using a contact pad in the palm of the glove. The other was a rapid-fire blade shooter that was made to rip through space-suits and the people wearing them.

The snap-pop sound of the ship's shield generator blowing out filled the cargo hold. They were firing on me. I momentarily connected to the ship's computer using the wireless within. The light frigate and its companion fighters had gotten ahead of the Uwebo while it was transitioning out of the atmosphere, and they were firing on the cockpit. I grabbed a hull cutter. It was an extendable metre-long arm with a laser installed at either end. I snatched a hand thruster from the armour crate and made sure that it was gassed up. I ordered my ship to stop accelerating then moved closer to the cockpit door. "You don't want this," I transmitted to her using the microphone in my helmet and the ship's comms system.

I turned my sensors up so I could feel everything around me. The air, the deck, my armour, the ship around me, the light frigate, which was lining up a shot that would blast the flight controls and the transparisteel above it. It felt like the universe was slowing down as I intentionally turned my processing speed all the way up. I used the connection to my ship to crudely fly it as though I was making another attempt to escape. "I will fire on you again. That cockpit will disappear."

"I'd rather you slag my ship than catch me," I told her. I wanted her to take the head off my ship. Her gunners were good. I could see they were lining their shots up just right to do it.

I waited on the safer side of the cockpit door as though I was trying to get away. The light frigate kept pace and position, keeping pace alongside. Seconds passed. They felt like minutes, then hours, and finally, someone pulled the trigger.

I let the explosive decompression push me through the doorway as the front of my ship was blown off.

CHAPTER EIGHT

Iteration

There was a glitch. It wasn't a bad one, but it was in my head and difficult to ignore. I'd only felt a glitch in my software once before, when a program that wasn't able to run until Alice's neural data was loaded into a digital system - my body - started up. That's when I went from thinking and acting like I was a normal human, to actually being self aware. This new glitch felt like a rebellious voice in the back of my mind and it was saying; "Turn all your scanners inward!"

I was trying to concentrate on what I was doing in space. Drifting faster than the headless hulk of my ship, surrounded by pieces of its bridge, I deactivated all of my life simulation systems. My body cooled down fast, and I turned the agonising sensation of that way down. Within a couple of seconds, I was aware that I was cold, but that was all. I hid behind a chunk of hull that I hoped would make it complicated for anyone on that light frigate to make my shape out.

I pointed my hand thruster, which used cold gas, so it would push me towards the frigate. It would look like some detached tank that had sprung a leak, I hoped. While I waited to close in on the light frigate, the Darmen One, I could feel that loud glitch in my program.

I pushed away from the chunk of metal I was holding to, and looked down at the hull of the Frigate. They were lowering their shields so they could dock with the surviving part of my ship. Most of it was intact, and a few compartments were probably still pressurised, so I'm guessing that Nera wanted to make sure I wasn't hiding in there.

I had never seen that model of Frigate before, so I had to guess that I was going to make contact somewhere near the crew quarters in the middle. I came down on the hull feet first, and the friction pads built into the soles of my boots clung to the hull. The grips were really made of tens of thousands of nano tendrils that could affix and release to match my steps.

I started gently walking along, avoiding portholes. If someone looked outside and announced; 'hey, there's a lady out there!' I would be screwed. I followed my sensors to the warmest part of the ship aside from the aft thrusters and saw the shape of a reactor in my readings. That was my destination. Engineering. Well, after I paid a visit to the bridge, which was also easy to find. I carefully moved towards the short conning tower. There were no portholes at the back, and only a couple on the side. This ship was made with pretty thick armour plating, but they kept the price of construction down by using as little transparent metal as possible.

The large ship seemed like a boring collection of rectangles, with too many large, flat sections. The cannons stuck out from ball turrets that seemed bolted them on wherever they fit. Like they were an afterthought. Two smaller multi-crew ships that were about thirty metres long moved into position ahead of the Frigate. Judging from their manoeuvring patterns, I guessed they were docking somewhere at the front.

I got to the back of the conning tower, climbed up as high as I dared, and then slowly clamped my hull cutter on. I was very careful to make all the impacts on the hull as light as I could so no one inside would feel the vibrations or hear a noise. Sure, there's no sound in the void, but something clanging and scratching the hull will make plenty if you're on the pressurised side. I extended the arms of the cutting tool so it would burn a metre wide hole and made sure that I could activate it remotely.

The glitch drew my attention to it even more as I moved down the conning tower and started making my way to the aft end of the ship. Finally, I interacted with the glitch and that shut it up.

I was sure that the glitch was a result of Bergio's patch. The way it manifested was a surprise, like I had this powerful urge to turn my attention inward, regardless of what I was doing. I followed its directions, focusing every scanner in my body towards my torso, and then I discovered something remarkable.

My specifications didn't include it at all. It was a well-protected and hidden piece of synthetic grey matter - an artificial biological brain that was about twenty-one centimetres long, five wide and two centimetres thick. It had its own life support, feeds for cooling, nutrients, and a thin barrier was wrapped around it that was supposed to keep it insulated.

It was amazing, about seven times as dense as a human brain, but it had suffered heat damage. It wasn't critical, but peripheral and there were signs of a little regeneration around the edges.

I'm no expert, I've never studied neurology or any of the related fields, but I guessed that there was burn damage.

I was still walking along the hull, paying attention to my surroundings as I asked myself the simple question: What is that thing doing, exactly?

It came to me all at once as though it had been holding the answer back since my creation. That was where my detailed personality lived and developed. It was my emotional core too, and, thanks to inadequate cooling and insulation, it had been going into stasis to protect itself whenever I turned my digital processing speed up. My processor cluster was nestled right under that bio-brain, so when it turned up, my grey matter would go to sleep, taking most of my personality with it. I turned my digital processor speed down to thirty-three percent and saw that my synthetic biological brain would be all right, even if I turned my body's warmers on and went into an atmosphere ideal for humans. I could live with that, but I would definitely need an expert to help me add insulation between my biological and digital minds in the future.

Sure, I could have used my internal regeneration systems to try to upgrade the insulation, but I couldn't find room for more. Even what the existing barrier was made of was a mystery, another super material.

As I walked along the outer hull, I thought back to the last time I'd made modifications to my systems. When I was still pretending to be Alice, a bunch of Order Officers nearly blasted me to bits. One of their shots found a flaw that shut me down, and I patched that up, making hasty changes to my design. I'm guessing that I created the problem then.

Before I could find someone to help, I had to take care of Nera and whatever other trouble I'd started. She also owed me a ship, my favourite gun, and my passport.

Darmen One, the Frigate, was finishing the docking sequence with the Uwebo. It irked me that they'd probably find a box with twenty-five thousand platinum in it along with a few other things that didn't get sucked out of the hold. That was about one hundred twenty-five thousand credits, enough money for me to miss.

I arrived at the dorsal docking port, and I avoided the pair of portholes on its left side. There was all kinds of information I wanted before going in there. I did not like going in guessing at the layout of the ship, who might be aboard, or even if there was another, bigger ship on the way. I decided to take a chance and look for available networks.

To my surprise, we were close enough to Greenfield Station to get a decent connection. Access only cost five credits, and they used a generic payment processor - Subo Pay - that would delete the details of the transaction as soon as it was over. I'd used them a few times, and verified that they delivered on their promise. I was just surprised that a legitimate station like Greenfield would use an alien company that was popularised by criminals.

I used my anonymous Stellarnet connection to look up and download all the promotional information about the Pinpai Manufacturing Security Frigate - the model I was standing on - and found the full Instruction Document. You know what they say; if you really want to know what you're doing, read the fricken' manual.

I dug into the Tabrus Government's records, their security was a joke, and saw that this ship, along with everything else the Darmen Corporation owned, was unregistered. A quick check with ship restoration companies in the solar system revealed that Darmen bought the ship a month ago from Tarbo Yards, a company with a reputation for reselling stolen ships. I got into their sales records and saw that the frigate I was standing on was the only one Darmen had purchased. That didn't mean it was their only large ship, but that was likely. Reinforcements wouldn't be on their way anytime soon, if ever. I turned all my attention back to the moment in time to see one of the star fighters getting closer. It was moving slowly, not directly at me but parallel to the Frigate.

I moved in a hurry, drawing a thin cable from my belt and connecting it to the door controls. I linked with the suit's systems and started hacking the door, trying hundreds, then thousands of passwords per second. As the fighter drew closer, I got desperate, and then I thought of trying the original manufacturer's default. I looked it up in the manual. The manufacturer's password worked! I couldn't believe it! Sure, it was a dorsal airlock that wasn't really accessible from the ground, but seriously? Who doesn't change that? I moved inside. Someone on the ship, probably on the bridge, noticed that the door was open and closed it, so I barely made it through.

I activated the environmental cycling system, and the airlock began to pressurise. I looked over my shoulder and saw that the fighter was moving past. Maybe it noticed me, that might have been why the outer doors closed so quickly.

Through the window in the internal hatch, I could see a pair of thugs in unweathered armour. They carried needle guns, the kind that could rip up most armour and do a lot of damage to flesh but little damage to a hardened hull. I put my hands up as the door slid to the side. The mechanism sounded flimsy, even cheap. I was seeing all kinds of places where the manufacturer of that ship cut corners.

I started the hull cutter that I'd left on the conning tower up. It confirmed that it had started burning a nice circular hole through the hull at the rear of the bridge level.

The soldiers in the hallway opposite the inner airlock doors raised their weapons and I put my hands up. "Step out of there," one of them ordered.

I did, still on cloud nine after figuring out how I could at least try to solve my dual mind problem. I also had a plan, one I liked maybe a little too much. "Take off the helmet," ordered the other soldier.

"What, his helmet?" I asked pointing at his partner without lowering my hands.

"No, you moron, Your helmet!" he snapped.

I did as he asked, and looked into his eye slit with a grin. "You don't think so now, but everyone here is about to have a very bad day. Take me to your Nera."

One of the guards cocked his head instead of answering me. The other regarded him urgently and then brandished his weapon at me. "Tell your raiding party to stand down, now!"

"You found them, huh? Where are they cutting through? The bridge, I bet. They're in stealth armour. You'll never detect them. They're going to kill everyone on the bridge and take control of the ship. You should surrender."

"Tell them to stop or I'll blow your head off!" the other thug shouted.

"I'm going to talk to Nera." I reached out quickly, snatching the underside of the nearest guard's helmet. Taking him off balance was as easy as yanking him towards me. Things got really bad for the guard when I kicked his feet out from under him and he went down as soon as I let go.

The other raised his weapon and I sidestepped, gripped his arm, then pulled and twisted. I didn't hear the cracking of a bone, but the creak of metal as he tried to fight me off. He was a cyborg.

At that moment I didn't want to kill anyone. My digital

computer system was working like a co-processor, giving me ideas on how to win the fight. It wasn't distracting, more like high-speed combat multiple choice. I grabbed the lip under the back of the cyborg's helmet, pulled backwards and down so hard and fast that I almost didn't get out of his way before he hit the deck. I heard the air rush out of him as he hit, and took that moment to steal his rifle. I pulled his helmet off with more care, revealing the face of a teenager. He blinked up at me, and I told him; "Start over. Get in an escape pod and fly away."

The other one got to his feet and brought his rifle up. He got a shot off, and it sparked off right my leg plate. I closed the distance between us before he could fire again and put all my strength into a single punch. I heard a sharp crack, and my sensors told me that I'd broken his neck. I turned on my heel and strode past the other hireling, saying; "Get out."

My next destination was the Reactor Control Deck. When my sensors confirmed that the young guard wasn't about to shoot me in the back, I ran for the Engineering section as hard as I could.

CHAPTER NINE

Trapping Trouble

Discovering that I had two minds - one that was good at being a person, another that was great at math and at running software - didn't mean that I had found balance. There was hope. I felt so much better thanks to my new understanding. There was something else, though.

As I took the long way to Engineering using the passages overlooking the ventral cargo hold, I thought about that. Balance isn't always good. It isn't always better. I felt whole, but the temperament of my digital side was mixing with the depth of feeling that I had thanks to that bio-brain. That feeling that I wasn't quite right was gone, so maybe that was the way it was supposed to be. I knew I wouldn't have snapped that guard's neck if I were calm, if my digital processor wasn't running at thirty-three percent. That was just high enough for it to add its own angry spice to my personality. I felt driven in a way I didn't before. I didn't know if I liked it yet, but I was sure I didn't want that to take over.

Alice had issues built up. Even before she became empathic, she had work to do, things to learn about herself. I know, this is a lot of talk about my feelings, but I'm just trying to say that I was realising that I wasn't at the end of a road but at the beginning. I thought about Jacob Valent then. He didn't go on about his feelings all the time. Not because he was perfect, far from it, but maybe I could try his method. By being myself instead of pondering why I felt the way I did all the time, maybe I could find out who I was.

I drew my blade-shooter and pulled my non-lethal anti-personnel handgun out from under my leg armour. I was careful to make sure the plates closed back up. I would try not to use the ripper blade shooter unless I had to. I came to the end of the main cargo bay and my sensors detected a large, unusual, cold shape.

I was running along a fortified catwalk that didn't budge under my quick footfalls, but it shook like it was about to collapse as whatever I detected dropped down in front of me. It was nearly twice my height, on two legs that looked like they'd been borrowed from some sort of cargo lifter, and it had flexible metal tendrils coming out of its elbows. Then I recognised the vital case, its torso. It was Ettin. His helmet was less decorative, with thick protective plating and no branding.

Faster than I expected, three of his tendrils whipped out and grabbed my legs. He picked me up and threw me into the main cargo area. I went down back first, bounced off the top of a shipping container, and finally fell spinning into an aisle leading down the middle of the hold. A hail of needle rounds came at me from each end of the lane between the piled crates and containers. This was his trap, they thought they'd take me out pretty easily, and they would have been right if I were human. The sound of the needles tinking against my armour filled my ears. Again, I was without my helmet, so the few hits they scored on my face bled convincingly, but there was no damage to anything beneath.

Anger, complex and invigorating mixed with alarm and frustration. I didn't dodge, or leap out of the trap. Instead, I aimed and fired two restraint rounds at a group of three cyborgs at one end of the cargo hold. The air shuddered as the rounds went off, instantly enveloping the trio in the same kind of alloy mesh that had ensnared me earlier.

"Call your attack on the bridge off!" Ettin bellowed from above in a voice that sounded low and inhuman.

My distraction, the cutting arm, was working well. They still thought that there was a team of invisible commandos on their way to the bridge. Their paranoia was going off. I didn't know how long it would last. The hope was that defenders were rushing to the conning tower, away from me and the engineering section.

I turned towards the opposite end of the cargo bay. Two cyborgs were firing at me sporadically. One of them was firing some kind of solid slugs. He'd missed for an entire magazine and was reloading. That was the problem with old-school slug throwers, you traded the number of rounds you could fire in one go for power. They also kicked harder than most weapons, so your accuracy would be terrible if you weren't ready for it. The other one was firing a needler attached to his wrist and missing most of the time. The few hits he made sparked off my armour, chipping at it but not penetrating yet. Then he caught me in the eye and it split apart like a grape with a firework at its centre.

A spike of pain made me wince and stumble. Sometimes the

simulation is too good. "Son of a bitch!" My eyes are amazing, but losing one is more of an inconvenience than anything. I have other sensors that make up for them, and I used them to aim and fire three suppression shells. They burst at the feet of my attackers, and the one with the big slug thrower was caught in the fibre mesh. The other leapt forward just in time to avoid it. I fired again and my non-lethal shell caught him in the face, instantly catching his entire body in its rapidly expanding, hardening plume. They wouldn't be a problem anymore, but I'd blocked the passage between the towering pile of shipping containers. Ettin leapt from the top of a cargo container. He was trying to drop right on top of me.

I moved back and fired at him with my blade shooter, dropping the empty suppression weapon. At my core, I'm an advanced combat android, so good aim comes naturally. By the time he slammed those giant feet onto the deck my ripper blades had severed two of his tendrils near the base.

I drew and fired the heavy pulse gun, sending a barrage of white energy bolts at his helmet. I wasn't taking chances with this metal beast. The rectangular helmet warped under the heat, and a seam started showing.

"No!" he shouted, flinging a tendril at me, reaching for the pulse blaster. I dodged it. I was starting to recognise that it was a pretty good weapon despite the requirement of an external power pack when one of Ettin's tendrils got behind me and grabbed the cable running from my arm to the back of my suit. He used it to draw me up off the deck, like someone picking a rat up by the tail, until I detached the line and threw my right glove off.

Two more tendrils came straight at me, trying to grab me by the head. I dodged them and jumped over him. Milliseconds before my feet touched the deck, three tendrils from his other arm flicked out and caught me by the waist. They closed with enough force to crack and bend my armour. I fired my ripper and only scored a few hits on his helmet before he shook me like a rag doll. "She wants you whole, but that won't stop me from breaking you on the inside," he said as he bashed my head onto the corner of a reinforced shipping container several times.

If I were human, my brains and chunks of my head would have been spread all over, but my skull was still intact. Metal was showing through which was more than a little annoying. He stopped and held me up to look at my half defleshed face. "I knew you were a cyborg."

That was a mistake. I aimed at the base of those tendrils with my ripper and opened fire. The blades tore at the flexible metal, severing two and leaving the last hanging limply. The material they were made of was better than flesh by far, but not nearly as hard as hull material. "Stop fighting, you idiot! I'm just here to square things with Nera!"

"I'm here to earn a bounty," Ettin said as a heavy hammer on a long arm folded out from his back and swung, catching me in the side of the head hard enough to knock me back into a shipping container. Before I could move out of the way it hit me again in the leg. My armour's left thigh plate was bent at an awkward angle. I fired at his helmet. Unlike the pulse blaster, my ripper didn't do any damage. A tendril wrapped around my wrist and tried to draw the gun off target.

"I'm not Alice!" I shouted as I affixed my boots to the deck, grabbed that whip like metal strand with both hands and pulled it hard. I forced him to bend down, his gears groaning, and I grabbed his helmet with my armoured hand while I rapidly punched it with the other using my bare fingertips.

After six hits, I'd opened the seam I saw earlier. I forced my hand inside enough to grab an edge. Ettin struggled as I yanked at the metal, tearing it open wider, revealing a brain case made of transparent metal. What was inside wasn't human, but a thing with three much smoother lobes. I put my hand against it. He stopped moving immediately.

"I'm so sorry, They make me do this. I'm kind, so kind. I will give you things," The words came through his vocaliser.

I didn't believe him for a nanosecond. I wanted him dead, but only because I was afraid that he'd come after me again if he survived. I had the advantage, few people would hold it against me if I followed through. It still didn't feel right. Killing because of some uncertain return felt like a cowardly, simple-minded thing to do. Instead I scanned his case and found the data converter that connected his brain to his body.

My inspection gave him a chance to make one more offer. "I have a ship. You can have it." A rectangular silver chip emerged from his collar.

I didn't let it distract me, but I wanted him to think he'd bought my mercy, even though my plan didn't change. "Thanks. That much buys your life, so I won't kill you. If you come after me again I'll cut you down and keep your grey matter in a jar in my common room." With my best threat in his mechanical ear, I pulled the little converter box free, sure that I wasn't detaching his grey matter's life support. His metal body slumped and clattered to the deck. I took the command chip from its slot and verified that it belonged to a ship, the Hinow-Sa, and he'd given me ownership, using my DNA code as the listed owner. It took a second for me to add my name and other details so I could scrub the code he used, which was correct, but would put the ownership of the vessel in doubt if I had to change again.

I was a mess. At least half the skin had been bashed off my

head, and my regeneration system was busy fixing a couple of dents in my skull. Wounds were sealing and some of my skin was re-growing thanks to an army of nanobots that used the little liquid reserve I had in my artificial digestive system.

I could sense fourteen more cyborgs and humans coming, running along the catwalks overhead. Tired of playing human, I leapt over the blockage I'd made when I caught cyborgs in metal mesh. My ripper tore into two thugs on my left before the magazine was empty. It took me about three tenths of a second to reload and I took three to my right down, cutting through one leg, a belly, and an under-arm.

My feet touched down on the uppermost cargo container. I dodged weapon fire and then leapt to the middle catwalk. Two crew members emerged from the forward hatch and fired at me with needlers. Another came through carrying a plasma cannon. That thing could do real damage to me at close range, so I ignored the first two thugs and shot the one carrying a cannon with a barrage of ripper blades. His neck was lightly armoured, so after two quick bursts it came apart.

The hatch sealed behind them and I leapt to another catwalk and landed nose to nose with a pair of crew members. One was a cyborg with polished metal limbs, the other was a shorter human in mechanised armour. The cyborg fired, catching me in the chest with his pulse rifle. That shot punched right through my armour. The air was filled with the smells of ozone, burnt insulation and skin. I grabbed his rifle and backhanded him in the head hard enough to turn his helmet to the right. His human companion tried to get a shot in, but I leaned and stepped around the cyborg, keeping it between us.

The chromed up thug clung to his rifle, as he punched at me with his other metal hand. I gave up on taking these two out. "Sorry, chrome boy, I've got somewhere to be and someone to see," I said as I leapt over and past him. When he turned around I stepped past the muzzle of his rifle and punched his vital case so hard that he not only stumbled backwards but clutched at his chest. As with most Cold Boys and Street Metal, there were vital organs in there. The deep dent I left in its middle probably scared him stiff.

His human friend wasn't giving up but he should have, because It took me an instant to push him over the railing. I looked at the cyborg, ducking a few needle rounds from my left. "The rifle. Give me the rifle or I'll bust you open."

He glanced down at what was left of Ettin and threw the rifle over to me. It was flashy, chromed like his arms and legs, but also a monster of a pulse weapon, made to vaporise armour plating at close range. If there were more cyborgs waiting, I would need it.

I nodded, slung the rifle and pulled the doors leading forward apart, breaking the latch holding them together. He watched, holding the dent I'd put in the middle of his chest.

Leaving him behind, I took the emergency ladder up to the engineering control deck and came up on two humans in green and gold corporate uniforms. They had their backs to the hatch. It was like they were trained in some video game, and not a good one.

When you're guarding an area, you should keep every door in front of you. They heard the hatch open, drew their sidearms and I split the last of my ripper rounds between them. They crumpled to the deck with horrific head wounds. A pretty uniform and a cap is never enough protection for your guards these days. Looking back on it, I killed them because I was impatient. I didn't look them up until they were on their way to the floor. After I found out that they were murderous wasteland thugs, I didn't care.

I let my digital computer run through all the known

members of the Darmen, checking criminal records and social media. There were nine people in the entire known gang that hadn't killed or enslaved someone and bragged about it at some point. The ones without blood on their hands joined after they tried to go corporate. I also found out that they owned the entire Ballistic Crush League, including all the teams. All that happened in seconds, it felt like I was getting a massive flood of information and I had to make a conscious effort to stop it.

As I shook my head, an older man in a heavy environment suit stepped in through a doorway, spotted me and ducked behind a terminal. "You're safe as long as you don't get in my way," I told him. "What's the security code for the power systems?"

"Promise I get out of here in one piece," he shouted back.

I looked at his reflection in the side of the countertop across from him and checked him out online. Pedro Odark was his name. Born Gail Odark, he'd been living as Pedro for six years, the last of which he'd been jobbing around as a Fusion Tech. That was the most interesting stuff about him other than a few fun vacation pictures of him on Gasema Beach. He was hired shortly after Darmen bought the ship. "You know where the lifeboats are," I replied, a little smile playing on my lips. "Can I have that code, please?"

He slowly reached under the terminal next to him and retrieved a note that had been stuck there. "This crew wasn't worth the pay anyway."

I saw it, tapped the sixty-four alphanumeric code into the computer, and made myself an administrator account. "Get going. Take anyone who you love with you." I said.

I connected to the frigate's internal network and assumed control. First, I turned the lights out. Life support followed. I wanted the crew to start counting the minutes before their air ran out, struggle against cooling compartments, and flail in a complete lack of gravity. To add one more reason for them to think about anything but me, I activated the radiological alarm and started a ship-wide announcement telling the crew to abandon ship.

CHAPTER TEN

Departures

Most of the crew were headed to the escape pods. Internal sensors, which were standard crap, so not super trustworthy, showed two hundred ninety souls aboard. That count was going down quickly, many of them not waiting until lifeboats were full before launching. Despite the glitchy internal sensors, I could see that my target and escape route were almost in the same place.

The Hinow-Sa - which loosely translates as 'Starlight Squid' - was docked with a forward mooring point. There was another ship there too, a touring ship called the Ring Skipper. The Officer Quarters were two levels above it, and guess where Nera was? Right there, opening an emergency hatch that would take her down a ladder to the forward docking ports.

I made my way there, running through corridors where

people barely noticed me as they ran for the nearest escape pod. I even passed two cyborgs who were fighting over one. "Geez, you can't share one?" I quipped as I passed. To my amusement, they stopped trying to pound each other into submission and got in together.

Taking a couple of service passages along the way sped things up. My digital side, which seemed to enjoy being connected to the Darmen One's internal network, noticed that someone was trying to get control back using the physical command chip, and they were about to win.

Before they could do it, I commanded every drive on the ship to erase themselves and then re-encrypt using randomly generated codes. The Darmen One was about to be as effective as a comet. The main bridge console didn't listen, but everything else did. Every other system on the ship was busy wiping its drives clean, which meant there wouldn't be software to run anything. Whoever was on the bridge would have to begin the software installation process, which would take manpower and a couple of days. That is, if they had backups at all.

The ship sensors went dead, a side effect of wiping software out ship-wide. I couldn't see what was going on using the security system, but my last peek showed Nera in the forward debarkation compartment shouting at a cyborg who was trying to hack the thick airlock doors. They were minutes, maybe seconds away from escaping aboard one of those ships.

It was easy for me to move through zero gravity, and before long I passed through a door into a broad hallway that led to the debarkation room. I moved to the door control panel, pressed my hand against it, sent a trickle of power to it, and then entered my administration code. It didn't work. The computer governing it was busy erasing everything on itself, so I had to pull the panel off and force electricity through the circuit that would force the motor to open the doors. The doors swept open, I detected Nera, and then she shot me in the head with my own Violator.

"Hell, yeah!" shouted Tony Rapson.

I could barely hear his voice over the sound of the thermite round trying to burn a hole through my forehead. The Violator is a great handgun against cybernetics, robotics and armour because it has an amazing initial punch that's followed by a compound that sticks and burns through its target. The sparks the reaction made lit the hallway up in fitful white and yellow. I let the metal piece that the round was burning detach and started to regenerate another small plate beneath it. I would need real mass to re-armour that three-by-three centimetre part of my metal skull, but a little protection was better than none.

"They said she was some kind of android, so..." Nera said before blasting me in the cheek and the forehead. That pissed me off. Worse, I was adrift, making no contact with the floor, walls, ceiling or anything else I could use for leverage. I dug at the sparking material digging its way into my skull as the human simulation gave me a muted taste of what it was like, and that was more motivation than I needed to scream and curl into a ball.

Why did I resort to theatrics? I couldn't reach Nera. I was adrift in microgravity with no surface within reach. Even if I stretched all my limbs out, I would have come up short. I admit, there are definitely downsides to being compact.

My head has some of the most sophisticated sensors you can find. There's also everything you need to perfectly simulate a mouth, eyes, ears, and a lot of other soft tissue features that I'm really attached to. She was burning pieces of me away and it pissed both my minds off.

Thankfully, other than a targeting system, no part of my

consciousness is in my head. Regardless of having new holes burned through my skull, I knew that the smartest thing I could do was pretend that those sparking rounds were digging into my brain, taking me out. There were more basic sensors in my chest and hips, so I wouldn't be blinded even if she took my head right off. Still, I lost my gravimeter, and then a trio of heat sensors that would be difficult to replace. I wasn't blind, but I only had one optical eye and other senses I really liked were disappearing.

Playing along, I twitched, clawed at my head, screamed, and worked as much of the active compound out of my wounds, burning the fingertips of my gloves. I managed to dig out some of it, stopping it before it burned through my metal cheekbone.

"God damn, is she a cyborg or some kinda android?" To my surprise, it was Synchron! He was walking right up to me, watching as I pretended to be in agony. My performance was convincing enough for him. "Come on, she's suffering. This isn't right,' he said.

"Get out of the way! If she's a cyborg, then there's a chance I'm only hitting sensors and emitters," Nera said, trying to push past him.

His eyes went wide, and he snatched the command chip for the Hinow-Sa, which had drifted free from my pocket. Then he let her pass. saying; "Don't destroy her, she's probably worth a fortune in parts!"

Nera wasn't stupid enough to get too close, and I was still drifting in the middle of the air, I wouldn't touch the deck for another thirty-four seconds. "So, maybe you're not Alice Valent, but I bet someone wants you. The question is, do I have to turn you in as scrap?"

I had to make sure she didn't notice me slowly drifting towards the deck, and I had an idea that my digi-brain would have passed up. "Ask Rapson. Hi, Tony, thanks for helping me out back at Headquarters."

The garishly chromed cyborg trying to wire a battery up to an airlock door panel looked over his shoulder at him first. "So, it's true? You sold an admin code?"

Nera and another executive in a blacked out helmet and matching plate armour that looked factory fresh turned towards him. "You piece of shit," came his distorted voice through his helmet's speaker.

Nera was next to offer a tongue lashing. "I thought your story was flimsy. This bitch isn't known as a great hacker, but she wins people over. What did she offer you in return for the admin codes you stole?"

"Nothing! I told you, I never had the access level she'd need to turn the 'bots against us. It was all hacking, she's lying," he replied, drawing his sidearm and putting his hand on a grenade that was strapped to his chest. "Let's get off this barge, and I'll show you again."

"You know, when the same accusation comes around again and again, there's got to be some truth behind it," Nera said. "And I've seen how she can wrap guys around her finger. I believe that more than..."

The hatch the cyborg was working on swished open as he finally connected the right wires to the battery. At the same time, I drifted close enough to the deck to plant my boot and the sole gripped the surface. It was enough for me to get leverage and lunge for Nera.

"Behind!" Tony cried. As Nera brought the Violator Seven around to fire at me. I already had her wrist in my hand as she pulled the trigger. A single shot fired into the ceiling and lit the compartment in sputtering yellow-white.

I'm not proud of what happened next. There was no pretence at human restrictions as I snapped her wrist like a graphite rod and watched her scream. "That's mine." I said as I took the gun out of the air before it could spin away. Shoving and locking it in my holster was satisfying.

"I thought you were Alice!" she screamed.

I planted my boots on the deck and they affixed firmly. "Where's my ID?" I asked, ducking behind her like a shield. Tony was trying to get a clear shot at me while the other executive was making his way into the airlock along with the cyborg who activated it.

"Not here. We use them to make fakes," she replied. "It's not too late, I'll have it brought here, then you can leave the system. We won't stop you."

My jaw clenched, and I leaned in until we were nose to nose. "What if I don't want to leave?"

For the first time I saw fear in her eyes, but my secondary sensors showed that her free hand was reaching for a small, powerful, two-shot disruptor pistol in a holster hidden under the back of her armour. "We'll work something out."

Her sheepish little smile was meant to placate me. She expected mercy, compromise, but I only saw a source of pain. Not just for me, but for the thousands she and her crew sold highly addictive narcotics to on Rodus, and everyone the Darmen Corporation would ruin in the future. Her low key glee at taking what was mine in New Zero would repeat as she elevated herself and revelled in using everyone she could. I whispered a warning even though I wanted her dead. "Give me a reason to end you."

The moment her finger brushed the weapon. In a quarter second I reached around her waist, grasped the gun, yanked it free from its holster and pressed the muzzle to her forehead. "Looking for this?"

Nera regarded me with real fear, frozen for a moment before whispering; "Who are you?"

"Look out!" Synchron shouted as he moved quickly, professionally, trying to bat the thing away. The helmet built into his vital case deployed, two halves coming up and joining, stiffening around his head as he moved.

As soon as his hand made contact, the grenade went off, blasting him through Nera then into me. It was the worst use of a grenade I'd ever seen. The compartment wasn't wide or tall, and everyone there was too close to avoid the pressure.

My face was a mess, so was my unarmored hand. The flesh was burned away from both for the most part. The skin did its job though, playing a part in protecting me from the heat and force of the explosion. I delayed regeneration since I was only missing two fingers, and I didn't strictly need my eyes yet. In retrospect, I'm glad I couldn't see the carnage around me.

Synchron's head and torso had come to rest against me. What was left of Nera couldn't be regenerated in the finest of medical centres. Tony Rapson wasn't spared either. It turns out that his flashy armour was more for appearances than anything else. He obviously didn't understand what a high powered grenade could do in an enclosed space, and he never would. The executive in the blackout armour along with the cyborg who opened the airlock were quick enough to get inside the airlock. My infra-red and radiological sensors confirmed that they were already on their way through the Ring Skipper's airlock.

Synchron's helmet split and retracted into his vital case's collar. His human-like legs and one arm were completely gone. "Hey, like that catch?"

I had a small group of nanobots build a tiny speaker in my throat so I could speak. "Thanks. I'd be worse off if you let it pass. Why did you do it?" I asked, pulling him upright by half an arm.

"I don't know if you noticed, but you dropped a starship command chip. I was hoping it would guarantee me a ride, but that's not worth a thing if you eat a grenade. I didn't think it would go off when I touched it, though. This is going to be expensive." He looked down as a small compartment built into his armoured core opened, revealing the command chip for the Hinow-Sa. "Gotta take me with, because I saved your life, right?"

"Deal," I said, taking the chip. I took a few seconds to check my Violator Seven and slid it back into its holster. The new scratches only added character. Nera's two shot disruptor was all right too, so it went into a pouch hanging on the back of my belt. There was nothing left of her. She was in normal clothing with a thin suit underneath, not enough to hold up to a grenade only two metres away, even with Synchron in the way.

The look that was on her face right before she died would never fade in my memory. There was no doubt in my digital mind that she had that and worse coming. My biological brain was satisfied that I'd prevented her from doing future harm to thousands, perhaps millions of people if she rose high enough. "Well, at least Nera didn't suffer. High powered grenades end things quick at close range," I said to myself, chuckling ruefully.

"Holy shit, what's wrong with you?" Synchron asked quietly.

"I'm still figuring that out," I said as I gripped his half arm and started for the airlock.

"I'm afraid to ask, but how'd you get Ettin to sign his ship over?"

"He traded it for his life," I replied as I ripped the control panel off the wall. The power cables for the inner airlock doors were right there, so I used my fingers to charge them, opening them.

"I wouldn't have believed that before, but now, well..." he started to say.

"Quiet. I don't know what's waiting for us in there," I said as I dragged him inside with me. I pressed the command chip up to the Hinow-Sa's airlock and was relieved to see it slide open. I used the connection to access its computer as I ran through carrying Synchron by what was left of his forearm. I pulsed my scanner, looking for bombs, traps, and anything out of the ordinary. There were three tiny trackers, but no bombs. "Okay, this is safe," I said to no one in particular.

"Really? How can you tell?" Synchron asked.

I was busy activating the ship's emergency de-coupling sequence, and any response I would have given would have been drowned out by the mooring collar's explosive bolts going off behind us. The Hinow-Sa started powering up as it drifted away from the Darmen One's forward airlock.

"Are you sure this ship is safe? I mean, you know Ettin's a psychopath, right?" Synchron asked.

"Even psychos keep a place where they can unwind," I replied, walking through the rear hold. It had been converted into a cybernetics workshop. At a glance, it looked like where Ettin designed and fabricated most of his parts. "Well, unwind and make repairs, upgrades. Looks like we can make you a few new parts."

"I knew you liked me," Synchron said. "Maybe there's a job at the end of this? I mean, you're going to need someone to..."

"Don't push it," I replied as I carried him through the ship, passing a turret access point and quarters with odd furniture. We finally arrived at the bridge, and I carefully sat him in a chair that looked more like the lower half of an eggshell.

"Rogue," said a voice through the emergency channel. "You're going to want to listen to me."

"It's Darman," Synchron gasped, wide-eyed.

I accepted his call and his copper coloured metal face appeared over the communications console. I'd never seen him before, his whole appearance was kind of surprising, and cheesy, as far as I was concerned, with blacked-out eyes and enlarged canines. "Someone's trying a little too hard to look dangerous," I told him. "I killed Nera. We don't have anything to talk about unless you're going to send my passport chip over. If not, I'll just report it stolen and move on."

"Nera would eventually come after my position, you did me a favour," he shrugged. "Now I need you to restore control to my ship."

"I can't. Every bit of data storage has wiped itself. You're going to have to try to restore everything from the bridge using backups, or call for help..." I explained as I started guiding the Hinow-Sa towards Greenfield Station using one and a half hands. I'm normally an adequate pilot, so I wasn't great with the handicap, especially since I couldn't sit. The pilot's seat was shaped like the lower half of an egg and too far back for me to perch on the edge.

"Then Bergio dies. It's too bad. He was a good tech," he said.

"Wait," I stopped the Hinow-Sa's acceleration, unsure of what to say.

"So, there is a way to restore my ship?" Vegol Darman asked.

I searched my mind and the Stellarnet for options and didn't find any quick way other than the proprietary Military Forced Flag Software that had been developed by Haven Fleet. I didn't have access to that, so it wasn't an option. There was no fast way to get his ship back online. "You'll have to restore..."

"We've already started that process. My expert tells me that it will take twenty minutes to regain thruster control. My fusion reactor isn't starting up because the only people left in engineering are morons who can't read a manual! Full reinstallation of software will take days. If you can't return us to full functionality, then Bergio dies."

I brought the Hinow-Sa around and activated the missile racks. Both of them reported ready. "Let me make this simple. If he dies, you die." I started looking for bounties online and found one. "The Sautoka Corporation wants you dead. I could use ten thousand credits." I fired a missile at the base of Darmen One's conning tower and watched as it went off, blasting armour plates free.

"He will die!" Vegol shouted.

"He's already dead," Synchron said behind me. "Darman doesn't hold back."

His tone was so hopeless that I believed him. "Let me see him! Prove that Bergio is alive!"

A tactical alert sounded, and I sent the ship into a dive, narrowly dodging a shot from the Darmen One's cannons. Someone managed to fire it manually from the turret. I looked at Vegol's hologram in time to see him sit down, resigned. We were in unpatrolled space, so far from Tabrus that there was no law to stop whatever was about to happen. Another cannon fired, striking the port side shields and doing superficial damage to the hull.

The ship I'd taken wasn't military, it wasn't meant to take the kind of punishment the kinetic cannons the Darmen One had. I programmed the navigation system with an erratic course meant to keep us out of the line of fire and concentrated on searching the Stellarnet for any reports of violent activity near Bergio's apartment. It took me less than fifteen seconds to discover that Siren Arms Security had already reported to a murder scene there, and found one male victim. I requested the DNA profile, paid fifteen credits for access, and compared it to what I already had on file. "You're a waste of life," I told Darmen as I confirmed that Bergio had been murdered. "Why even tell me about Bergio if you already killed him? I was about to fly away, leave your trash frigate twisting in my exhaust."

"You already know? How did you check so..." Vegol said in surprise.

"You shouldn't try to hide anything from the one who nearly tore your organisation on the ground apart for putting me in a box and taking my stuff. Bergio was a friend. A pacifist, and he didn't deserve what your people did to him."

"Who are you to decide what anyone deserves?" Vegol asked. "He installed cybernetic power in murderers for years. No one is innocent. Now fix my ship!"

"Maybe someone should make decisions about people like you more often. I'm still figuring myself out, but I think I'll try it." I was feeling something powerful, an urge that reminded me of the Overlord II, and what I did to Vindyne staff after I saw them sending people to labour camps and laboratories. I passed judgment on employees and freed as many innocents I could by creating chaos on their base ship. Then I freed myself by becoming human. My morals weren't pinned down then, and they felt malleable again as I got a missile lock on the Darmen One's bridge.

"Wastelander trash like you doesn't deserve to even speak to me. I won't be judged by a scrap rat who pretends to be human. I see what you are; just metal. Join us, we'll make you feel power-ful, give you wealth for your violence." Vegol spoke as though he was looking down on me from a throne.

"Didn't the Holocaust Virus teach you to be careful when

you're talking to metal?" I knew exactly how many I'd need to break through the bridge, and where the missiles needed to hit.

"Launch one missile and make enemies out of every new organisation coming out of the wastelands," Darman said, sitting back. "You won't survive long."

"At least one planet will be better off without you," I replied, pulling the sideways triggers for the Hinow-Sa's missile racks. I'd set the tactical guidance system up so they arranged themselves in a line of twenty-three projectiles. They struck the same spot on the transparent steel bridge window, one after the other. It took eleven hits to penetrate. The rest flew through the hole, detonating inside the bridge and in the hallway behind it. Vegol Darman may have had enough time to get out and run down the hallway. I hoped the missiles I sent to the back there got him. I swept the conning tower with scanners and saw a few people moving around near the base.

A cannon fired, striking the aft side of the Hinow-Sa, and I had to get us out of there. As we accelerated away, my passenger asked; "What happens to me now?"

"I don't know, Synchron. What do you want?" I asked, not turning to look at him.

"I'm a pretty incomplete unit here. Would be really nice if I had your kind of regeneration tech, wow, you're almost a knockout again," he chuckled. "Seriously, though, I'm hoping you don't toss me through an airlock. Oh, and my real name's Chuck. That's funny. I'm afraid you'll space me, you know, chuck me."

"Well, I can't trust you, so you're getting left at Greenfield," I replied. "They have a hospital there, a service centre, and you have credits, right?"

"Not that many. Darmen Corp controls my accounts. Maybe

something's spend-ready, but..." he shrugged and started to fall over.

I caught him and made sure he was sitting upright. "I'm not going to take you in. You're not a stray." I remembered Mimi then and realised I'd have to tell her that Bergio was dead. . "I should space you, but you're getting dropped off somewhere warm, with air. Thank me."

"Thanks," he replied quietly, averting my gaze.

CHAPTER ELEVEN

Repairs

The Hinow-Sa's interior wasn't upgraded in the least but there were plenty of modifications that I'd discover later. None of them would be what I call convenient or useful. Ettin had made the ship into an oddity, and I knew it would take me forever to sell it to an individual.

There wasn't even a record of what race Ettin was, so I couldn't search for his people to see if any one of them wanted it. I registered it with the Tabrus Government and the Navnet Network, which would mark the ship as mine across the galaxy eventually. There was a conflict with an ownership claim in New Zero's database. It said that Ettin bought it from a salvage lot, but I put a counter-claim in that would muddy the waters. That was a common thing, since there were several salvage companies that went looking for abandoned or crashed ships that were in good shape, dusted them off, and then sold them. Until corporate salvage outfits hit Tabrus a couple of months ago, good salvagers were finding working ships fairly regularly.

I reached down the neck of my shirt and tucked the command chip into my bra. It was the size of my pinky nail. "Why aren't we there yet?" Synchron asked, the painkillers in his system causing a little slur in his speech.

"I'm taking us to regulated space. We'll let Navnet guide us to Greenfield. If someone jumps us on the way, I want the right people to see it," I replied, re-checking my course. Once I was sure that we were going the right way, I locked the controls and headed for the workshop.

"Smart. Let the fighter jocks work for you. I guess you own this weird tub now?" he asked as I passed him.

"Sort of, but not for long. There are a few traders who will give me something for it. Maybe I'll throw you in as a sweetener," I replied.

Synchron laughed, then stopped abruptly. "Wait, you wouldn't would you?"

I let his question hang in the air for a moment, and then I had a thought. I didn't know that he was actually immobile. For all I knew he had something hidden in his torso that could walk him around, like a few tiny legs or a miniature hover drive. I picked him up, found a closet with some cleaning supplies inside, made sure that there was a safe corner for him, and put him in. "See ya when we get there," I told him as I closed the door and locked it.

"Oh, seriously? I've got one arm and no hands. What am I gonna do? Pirate the ship with my teeth and clever talk?"

"I've gotta keep what's left of you safe so you can get back in the arena," I quipped back.

"There's not much of a league left. Taking Darmen Corp out

was bad for the sport since they owned the whole goddamned thing here!" he shouted after me.

I looked around in the workshop and found a locked cabinet. I broke it open and found what I was looking for. Rare pure materials in dust form made for fabrication systems. I perused the selection of transparent tubes, picking a few up as I compared them to a list in my head. My repair systems could work miracles, even turn energy into small amounts of dense solids if I had access to enough, but it was easier to grab what my repair system was asking for instead. I found mulite that I'd combine with titanium to rebuild pieces of my skull. I only needed half a gram of xanit so my skin could refract scanners, tricking them into seeing a human body using special refraction and micro-structures. I took all ten grams, you know, just in case. Finally, I took Kymium, which would coat any repairs I made to my metal parts to help them regenerate if I ran into trouble again. There was no nidrium, so my gravimeter couldn't be rebuilt to the same standard, but I was sure that there was a less accurate spare lying around in a parts drawer. After a brief search, I found one that was about a quarter as effective, but it would do in a pinch since it was the right size.

I started dumping the powders and fine flakes into a jar of restorative gel along with some common compounds. As I did that, I called Lat, making sure that our connection was audio only. He answered right away and I heard Mimi in the background. "Tell her it's boring here because you won't let me out!"

"Hello, Rogue. We're here. No one followed us," Lat said. "Is it supposed to be empty?"

"Empty? No. There should be supplies, a Saga Maker and some other stuff," I replied.

"What's a Saga Maker?" he asked.

"A really expensive fabricator. I was lucky to find it in one piece." Hearing that the bog cache had been robbed was disappointing. What I found in the cargo hold of the Hinow-Sa didn't make up for half of it. "So, there's no food, no safe?"

"Nothing. We're sitting on the floor. It's dry and warm. That's good. I bought Mimi some food on the way in, and I've got bars. We can filter water."

My gemstones were in there along with about seventy thousand platinum. The platinum alone would have been worth a little over three hundred fifty thousand in local credits. I was getting poorer by the hour. Worse, there was only one more hidden cache that I set up for humans other than The Pit. If that was scraped clean, then I owed more than I had in raw currency. "I'll be there in half an hour."

"What about Darmen?" asked Lat.

"Their fighters scattered when I shut their ship down, but they still have people on the ground. I'll get to you faster if I can."

"I'll watch the perimeter from cover. Is there room on your ship for the hover car? I like the one I got, and it was a good deal."

Lat's concept of money was a little loose, to say the least. I looked around and nodded. "There's room for a four-seater." There was a glut of hover cars in dealerships and scrap yards around the planet because they were too easy to find in the wastes. Most of them were in pretty good shape, too, so all but the most impressive hover vehicles were going for a credit and a song. My bike was one of the more impressive hover vehicles I'd seen. I knew I'd miss it. It cost almost nothing to operate, too.

"Good. We'll be ready," Lat said, ending the call.

I looked at the thick, gooey mixture I'd made on the bench. It was one point one litres of restoration gel along with all the powders and flakes I'd added. I started downing the stuff, gulping it down, and my material management system got to work. It tasted like copper, burnt wood and something earthy. Humans could drink restoration gel, but it wasn't recommended. It was really a topical kinda thing, but my systems would use it to repair all the synthetic flesh damage I'd taken.

The nanobots started with damaged metal though, and I sighed as whole chunks of my skull were rebuilt in a couple of seconds. Healing feels good. It's a relief, there can be tingling, and a feeling that things are being set right again. My eyes were fully remade next, and flesh followed. I looked in a big mirror and saw that my hairdo could use a lot of work. I pictured Ayan Anderson and, after my face was finished, I grew a thick mane of red ringlets with a live core. It wasn't real hair, but biological hairdo's weren't in fashion then, and it looked like the genuine article. The least authentic thing about how it looked was that it wouldn't tangle unless I wanted it to. It also added an extra layer of armour.

The whole repair process took a little less than eight seconds because of the raw materials I'd taken in, and I felt so much better. I ran to the cockpit. I was within Tabrus' Navnet's control range, so I requested the quickest course back to the lower hemisphere. I didn't specify which continent I wanted to come down on, just in case someone was reporting my movements. They gave me a nice, straight course and I pushed the ship's main thrusters as hard as I dared. After programming the autopilot, I rushed back to the workshop.

Eating and drinking human food is fun, I enjoy it, and my repair systems can use water along with other solids to take care of most critical damage. Sadly, a vegetable wrap and a glass of water put my matter conversion system to work, slowing the repair process down a lot. Pure, dense materials that are closer to what I need, requiring no conversion are better. Not nearly as tasty, but better. Since I had access to all those high quality materials, I mixed a bigger batch of that thick repair goo, downed another litre that would stay in my digestive system until I needed it, and then poured the rest into unmarked containers that I threw into a backpack. There was enough stuff there to rebuild half my body, and I would start getting a bulge if I stored more in my stomach.

By the time I was finished, the Hinow-Sa was about to enter the atmosphere, so I took the controls and took it the rest of the way to my swamp stash. As I burned across the sky as fast as Navnet would allow, a call came in. The signal was coming from Bergio's address. I accepted it and was given access to the apartment's security system. At a glance, I could see the surgery area, where Bergio's body was still splayed on a procedure table, opened from neck to leg. It looked like someone played with him, and then cut his head off. I moved on to check the surveillance feeds in the other rooms.

The place was abandoned, cordoned off by orange plastic sheets with CRIME SCENE printed on them. Like that was going to keep anyone out. As I wondered how many people knew about Bergio's parts room, filled with new and used cybernetics, I noticed that one of the video sensors - a very good one - was pointed out a window. It was focused on a pair of cybernetic thugs who were in a living room across the way. A pair of Obrun, a large-eyed, stout race with dark fur and thin fingers that barely peeked out past their forearm down were sitting in the corner behind them, terrified.

Another cyborg was sitting on the balcony, drawing on a vaporiser stick. As he exhaled a long white cloud, I looked his face up in the Darmen Employee Database. The public-facing part of the site had him listed as a Resource Acquisition Officer.

His legs and Vital Case were military grade, while his arms and helmet looked like thickly armoured custom pieces.

I didn't know who was calling from Bergio's apartment, but they were either warning me not to go there or asking me to take care of these three. I was able to pan the video sensor a little, and then zoom through the window into the living room. What I saw then set my teeth on edge. One of the cyborg thugs on the other side of the window was helping another install Bergio's arm into his shoulder socket. They were having trouble. I couldn't hear them because there were thirty metres and two window panes between the audio sensor and them, but I could see that they were arguing. Every time one of them yelled, the Obrun in the corner behind them flinched. I didn't need much more reason for an intervention.

Bergio was a pacifist, but I wasn't. It might have been a trap, but sometimes you can turn a trap around if you know about it in advance. My viewing was interrupted as I checked my Government Email. It was a habit. When I could freely stay on the Stellarnet without worrying about being found I used to check messages every few seconds. I found job offers and a few other messages from corporations and a few other organizations. I was still connected to Greenfield station's network, so I switched to an anonymous terrestrial account instead.

I took face captures of the cyborgs who were watching Bergio's place and used them to look up a police file, hoping that Siren Arms had publicly named them as killers. They had. There they were; Yabrik Skyl, Hovan Skyl and Zord.

Zord was the one who I'd spotted on the balcony, the other two were brothers who were employed by the Darmen Corporation. The evidence in Bergio's apartment had been collected, analysed, and the court program convicted them of murdering Bergio. There was a public notice ordering them to turn themselves in. A HATE notice had been issued on them with a reward of fifty thousand credits each. It was the first HATE notice I'd ever seen. I had to look it up. It meant Hunt and Terminate, which was a bit of a stretch to make an acronym, but I understood why they did it that way. You would never mistake a HATE notice for being anything but a bad thing.

I tried to look into the bounty but I was taken to a site with the image of an armoured Goddess in the middle. She was carrying a heavy sword and shield and her helmet was up, revealing a face that was angelic, but pale marble, along with the rest of her skin. I backed out of the site, and looked at the bounty markers more closely. The Government had sent the bounty to Themis, a Task Broker company. I was surprised to see that they weren't simply a bounty broker, but specifically a company that handed jobs of all kinds out. If you needed something legal done, Themis would try to find you someone who would do it.

I looked at their site again, and was denied entry no matter what I tried. Finally, the Goddess looked at me and said; "You are using an anonymous connection. We can't do anything for you unless you tell us who you are. A Standard Identification Number would do nicely."

I considered revealing myself. I had a valid Ident. My passport chip may have been gone, but the Identification Number behind it was still valid online. I needed to know more about this company first, and I started searching as quickly as the Stellarnet connection I was using would allow. Themis was first formed two hundred seventeen years ago by Klynn Costas, a bounty hunter who was operating in wild territories. She built the organisation up over several decades before disappearing. The company folded about twenty years after her son took over.

Themis was restarted several times since then, and expanded

into an odd job company as well as brokering bounties, providing a large board with a variety of work types. It allowed them to provide work wherever you were, regardless of how lawless your environment was. If you were in a solar system where crime was under control, you could haul cargo, provide transportation, join an escort team, or find technical work.

If you were in a lawless area, you could still find work under all those categories and go after bounties. They had just started the local chapter of their operation a few weeks ago, and I couldn't find any problems. They were also in talks with Haven Fleet to support their fight against the Order of Eden. It looked like they were going to pay people to take Order troops out, capture or destroy their equipment, and put big bounties on specific people in the corporate cult.

As a final check before contacting them again, I tried to find out who was already working for them. Other than a couple of conspicuous hunters who bragged on the Stellarnet about their captures, I couldn't find a thing. They were rising in popularity, though. It turns out that Themis' bounty boards were partially public. Bounties that were pending didn't show who the targets were, or if anyone was in pursuit. That was secure.

The Execution Board was a different story. Targets that had been captured and submitted to the authorities or a Themis Complex were listed, and hunters could make themselves visible, so everyone could see who cashed the bounty in. They also listed the visible hunters in a ranking order, and the fact that the top five as well as many others didn't allow their names to be listed publicly didn't escape me. I wondered if Jacob Valent had experience with similar organizations, and what he'd say about going public or staying private.

For the time being, I was happy to see that Themis was a discreet organisation and more than a middle man. They owned several companies already. Osiris Shipyards, Green Spark, and Spectral Dynamics. Two of those companies were re-headquartering on Tabrus.

The last thing I did was check the Local Matrix for my name. There was a chance, though very slim, that if I was on Themis' bounty boards, that it would leak into the pool of knowledge used by hackers and search programs. There was no evidence that I was wanted, so I gave their site my Ident.

The site verified it, asked me a couple of questions like where I applied for my Ident, what my last port of call was, and the name of my first registered ship. I was in after that and immediately shocked when Fi-Bank sent me a message informing me that I had earned a reward for the confirmed kill of Erraxin, a cyborg aboard Darmen One. I had no idea who they were talking about until I checked my Themis details and saw the playback of one of the ship guards on the catwalk catching several of my ripper blades under the nose. His bounty was worth ten thousand, and there was a five thousand credit tip on top of that from an anonymous source for the trouble I'd caused the Darmen corporation. It was like found money, and I felt fine about it since Erraxin was a convicted murderer.

"Welcome to the Themis organisation. We'd like to meet you," said a very masculine voice. "You've been approved as a hunter because our vetting team sees you're capable and already pursuing members of a corporation that local law enforcement has marked with several HATE notices."

"How did you find the footage from Darmen One?" I asked.

"Another contractor is already processing that ship and arresting survivors. They're uploading footage to our base now. Tabrus is eager to get the wreck cleared. This situation is moving fast, and we're interested in acknowledging your work," the voice replied. "It is our way."

"I didn't contact you to claim credit. I'm not here to boast," I said, determined to stay on task. There were lives at stake, and I wanted to avenge Bergio. If it weren't for him, I wouldn't have figured out the first step to putting my personality together. I may have cooked my grey matter for good, too. I owed him a lot. "I see HATE notices on these targets," I said as I highlighted the profiles I found on Yabrik Skyl, Hovan Skyl and Zord.

"Three bounties. Difficult targets. Why contact us at all? Killing an outlaw isn't against the law," the voice said.

"I was making sure these three were criminals. If the law cared about protecting them, I'd have to be a little more careful," I replied.

"So, you fight to avenge," a sonorous female voice concluded.

"No," I replied, aware that it wasn't true as I said it. I didn't have to ruin the Darmen One to get to Nera. I didn't have to turn and fire thousands of credits worth in missiles at the light frigate. I didn't have to avenge Bergio. "I like balance."

"So do we," the male and female voices replied in harmony. "There are bounties on all three of your targets. The hunt is legal. Siren Arms is paying because they don't want to put their law enforcement personnel at risk. Considering their criminal history, Themis sanctions their destruction or capture. The laws here are simple. Announce yourself and give them an opportunity to surrender. Record your actions, otherwise you won't be credited. Do not knowingly harm civilians or outsiders. The collateral damage may not exceed the value of the total bounties earned on site."

"That's it? I expected a million-word rulebook," I said.

"There is one more point, but it's not a rule," The female voice said. "If another hunter arrives, you are not obligated to work with them, but it's encouraged."

"Is anyone else after these three right now?" I asked.

"Normally we wouldn't say," said the male voice.

"In this case, it's safe to say that you'll be alone. No one is touching this," said the female.

"Thank you," I said, waiting a moment and then ending the call. I received a temporary Themis Operating Code. This had become a legal hunt, and I would be going after targets that official law enforcement wasn't willing to take care of. It felt good.

CHAPTER TWELVE

Bad News

I put the ship down about a kilometre away from the swamp cache and opened the workshop doors. There was a ramp that was large enough for a hover truck or shuttle, so the car would fit after I moved a couple of workbenches. When the squarish hover car Lat bought came in, I was servicing my Violator Seven sidearm with a couple of new parts I'd printed. The fabrication machine was at work beside me, making extended magazines along with my custom ammunition. These rounds were barely legal killers, made specifically for Yabrik Skyl, Hovan Skyl and Zord.

Zord was Darmen Corporation's Chief of Operations. Before they tried to go official, when they were just a wasteland gang, he was Darman's right-hand man. A sky raider, and a town razing slave trader. Yabrik and Hovan Skyl were brothers who did whatever he told them with a combined body count that was nearly four digits according to the evidence they left on social media.

I knew coming in from the wastes would be difficult, that I'd have to get used to Tabrus having millions of people around, but I didn't expect to see gangs that tried to evolve into corporations. Especially while they left evidence on the Stellarnet for anyone to check out. I finished checking my Violator and put it in its holster.

The car door opened and Mimi dropped to the deck, took a few steps and had a long stretch. Lat came out after, taking her bag and a couple of shopping sacks out before closing the door. The car slowly lowered to the deck to settle on tiny resting wheels. "See? I told you she'd pick us up in something suitable."

"I said something nice. This looks like Bergio's lab, only with worse machinery. That one's not even properly cleaned," she said, walking around. "Is he here?"

"No," I said, trying to hide the pang of sympathy I had for the cat as she came over to me. "But this ship is safe for now. We'll be getting something nicer soon."

"Bergio told me that bigger and better aren't the same things. So I hope you don't mean bigger," she advised.

"Nicer either way," I said, looking at Lat, who was watching both of us.

"You are very tense and have changed your appearance. I think it's your hair. I don't see your jacket, either," he stated.

Mimi looked at him, then up at me, raising a paw. "So curly, let me touch," she said playfully.

I didn't want to do what came next, but keeping Bergio's death from her didn't make sense to me. There was no doubt that he was gone. No way she would want to see what was left. The ramp finished raising and the aft doors clanged closed. I knelt down and she sat, collecting herself. "I have to tell you something."

Lat's eyes were on me, narrow and wary. Mimi shifted on her haunches and asked; "What's wrong?"

I didn't know what I said for certain until the words were out of my mouth. "You know I took Bergio seriously, right? When he told me to take care of you? I will. You have a home, even if we switch ships sometimes. I'm going to take care of you."

"Okay, good to know. Especially since that lummox doesn't always listen to me," Mimi said, glancing at Lat. "But what's wrong? Tell me."

"Bergio is gone." I don't know why I said it that way. Well, I think I was trying to spare her feelings with inference, but I know better.

"Where? Can we go see him?" Mimi asked.

"She means that he's dead," Lat said.

Mimi turned and hissed at him before returning her attention to me. "No, that's not what she said! He's okay, he just went away!"

"I'm sorry. Someone killed him. I'm going after them," I told her as softly as I could.

Mimi immediately started cleaning herself by licking her paw and then drawing it down over her face, something she repeated until I reached out with a soothing hand. I was surprised when she lashed out, scratching me hard enough to draw blood. My skin was only simulating the injury, but I got the point. Without a word, she bounded off into the ship. "I was trying to soften the blow," I told Lat.

"It wasn't working. Soft or hard, death is death," he said.

I could have shot him then. That guy isn't made for subtlety, and there are moments when he just gets on your nerves. I saw that he'd bought her kibble and canned food, so I printed a bowl for her with her name on it, and a water dispenser that would act like a little fountain with a falling stream of water when she went close to it. "Go check the cockpit. See if you know how to fly this thing."

"All right," Lat said, pushing on the car to make sure it was locked down before he left.

I used my sensors to find Mimi, who was in a strangely shaped chair in the crew quarters, cleaning herself. She was so small that she could fit in the middle of the seat comfortably. I put the bowl and water dispenser down by the door, filled them and then looked at her. She had her leg straight up as she continued to clean herself as though she'd been rolling around in the bog. She was pretty clean already though. "I'm sorry. I wish I'd stayed and saved him."

"So do I!" she shouted back. "What were you doing instead? What was so important?"

"I thought they were just after me. I was drawing them off so they'd ignore him. I'm sorry," I replied.

Without another word, she went back to cleaning herself. I opened the can of Tempting Tuna and scooped it out into the sub-compartment built into her kibble bowl. I licked my finger then, probably a leftover instinct from Alice, and was surprised to find that it tasted pretty good even though it was synthetic fish. "It's there if you get hungry. I'm going hunting today, so I'll be going off-ship. I'll check on you before I leave."

When I got to the cockpit, Lat regarded me from the controls. "I switched this over to Standard Human Interface, but there's nowhere for me to sit. I tried that chair but it's too far from the dash and there's nowhere for my legs. I don't like this ship. Oh, and there's someone locked in the closet."

When Lat had something to complain about, he had no filter and no sense of when he should stop. On top of a fuzzy Kawaii Kitten who was furious at me, it felt like I was doing everything wrong, and I couldn't shut my emotions down anymore, so I just shook my head. "I'm gonna trade it in before my ownership is contested, hopefully. The Envoy should be back soon if it got through all the waypoints without getting slagged."

"Oh, that's your other ship," he nodded as though he didn't believe it was real.

I let it go. Maybe the suggestion that he didn't believe the Envoy was real was all in my head, there was a lot going on in there. I told him about Synchron, how I got his ship, and what I was doing next as we lifted off and I took the controls. After I finished telling him about Themis, he turned to me and said; "I want to join."

"Contact them. They'll have to vet you, and you need an Ident that clears."

He shifted on his feet and clenched his jaw, looking insulted, like I made the rules. "You know I don't have one. I can't even pay someone to make one for me. My DNA disqualifies me because thousands of soldiers have it."

We were coming up on Errade City and I was a little low on patience. "Even if I could take you with me on this one, I wouldn't because I'd be afraid of what would happen if this thing got knocked off." I tapped one of the small emitter rods coming from the scrambler ring on his head. "The Order might detect you, send a signal out. They could regenerate you behind my back. Not a risk I can take while I'm going after combat cyborgs."

He recoiled for a moment. "I can't help what I am."

"Yes, you can! You can take this pill, regenerate on your own terms and leave all that framework shit behind. No framework, no risk, full control. Do you understand yet?" I shouted, letting my frustration get the better of me. It was the first time. Well, the first time I really lost it at someone I liked. I was feeling more human all the time, but I can't say that was always for the best. "Take us to these coordinates, get down to four hundred twenty metres, wait for me to jump out, and then land outside the city. I'll call for you when I'm done."

"What if I just left?" he asked.

I waved the comment off and left the three-seat bridge. "I have to get ready."

If he left, I'd have to track him. I felt responsible, knowing that at any moment that scrambler could fall off his head and the Order of Eden could take control again. Then I'd have to kill whatever kind of soldier they fabricated using the system built into his bones. I didn't want them to get the slightest toe-hold on Tabrus, especially if it was because I took sympathy on a deserter.

I put that out of my head, took the new jacket I'd printed out of the machine and put it on, drawing the hood up. It wasn't as well armoured as I liked, but it would have to do. I put the chest sections and the arms of my armour on over it. It was in pretty bad shape, with burns across the chest and the right pauldron, but I wanted the protection. I straightened a couple of the armour plates on the lower half of the armour using a stationary bender and roller that did a cleaner job than I would have with my hands. It looked like I'd been through a war already, and the repairs had a hasty quality to them. The magazines and ammunition were finished fabricating, so I put all ten of them into the belt I'd made along with three electromagnetic pulse grenades I found in a large weapon crate that was empty otherwise.

I re-checked my sidearm and holstered it. We were almost

there, and I was ready, so I peeked in on Mimi. She was eating the tuna like she expected someone to take it away. "I have to go. I'll try to be back soon." She didn't acknowledge me.

I wanted to say I was hunting the people who killed Bergio, but didn't. Instead, I checked on Lat. "I hope you're still around to pick me up. It would be a long walk through Errade back to the ship."

"I will be," he said quietly. "We're almost over the Stanley building."

I started for the rear ramp.

"I still don't know what to do with the guy locked in the closet!" he called after me.

"Leave him there, no matter what he says. It's better for everyone," I replied over my shoulder.

I lowered the rear ramp, watching the ship's status in my head. Lat got us clearance to fly over the city and we were moving in a straight line. Lat was a functional pilot, even though he thought he was amazing, but I had no complaints then because he was following instructions. He kept us at the lowest altitude allowed, and I watched the tops of towering buildings go by below. One of the larger ones was on fire, the top ten or so stories bathing the shorter buildings in yellow-red light like an old match. We were close to the lawless sectors of the city and I wondered if I'd end up venturing in there if I took more bounties.

For the last time, I considered what I was about to do. Themis was a go-between, a company that took money from governments that wanted punitive action taken and paid people to carry that out. I was volunteering to do that against people that I was sure had it coming. If things went as I expected, anyone would be justified in calling me a paid killer even though I planned on offering them the opportunity to surrender.

I stood at the edge of the ramp, watching the tops of buildings go by mentally searching for one more thing that would put me in the 'good guy' column. Both my minds were united on what that was. *These criminals have done harm, and they will do worse if they continue to cultivate power.* I stopped questioning myself and what I was about to do.

CHAPTER THIRTEEN

The First Bounty

The few stories Alice heard about her father's bounty hunting years stuck in her mind like legendary tales. Jacob Valent was professional, business-like, and well he made sure he was well equipped for most of his career. Jake kept his crew fed and ship, the Samson, flying but he didn't always like the jobs he had to take. Jacob Valent was a well known hunter by the time he moved on to other things, but I imagined the job I was on would have been one he would take with a grin. Maybe if conditions were different, Alice would have gotten into bounty hunting, but that road was mine, and it felt right.

My grin was on the inside. As I hit the roof and rolled, it was as if I was following in Jake's footsteps. I felt like I was five meters tall, powerful and filled with purpose. A startled ship maintenance worker turned and watched me pass, holding a hose in both hands. The rooftop landing pads were home to three starships, all nice enough to steal, so a pair of security guards at the far end of the roof turned towards me, holding a hand up as they kept the other on their Rippers. "Hold up there," one said.

I stopped, but my scanners were looking past them. The building where Zord and the brothers were holding up was behind them. "Hi, I'm on the job."

One guard snickered and shook his head. "In that armour? Did you find it under a scrap pile?"

My sensors reached out and I focused in on the apartment across the way and five floors down. Zord was inside, sitting at the head of a table with Yabrik and Hovan Skyl. The Obruns didn't seem to have any cybernetics installed. The large-eyed marsupials definitely weren't with the trio I was after. Even though I didn't know much about Obruns, I was pretty sure their high heart rates suggested that they were terrified.

The guards were staring at me, so I flashed a smile. "I've tracked a bounty to a building near here."

"Oh, you're serious, little girl? You're going after a bounty? You're not even wearing a helmet," one of the guards said.

"It's not in this building, is it?" the other guard asked more seriously.

My infra-red sensor gave me enough detail so I could see Zord push something - maybe a plate - away from one of the Obrun. He shoved her out of her chair then, and I decided it was time to get past these guards. "This has been fun, don't get in the way," I said as I leapt over them, landed close to the edge of the rooftop, got a running start and jumped across the six lane gap between the buildings.

It felt like I was in the air forever as I waited to land across the way. Something one of those guards pointed out did get into my head though. Once again, I'd forgotten my helmet. I'd have to work on that in the future, it was a bad habit. My feet touched the roof, I rolled, and came up running. The windows of the apartment Zord and his lackeys were holed up in faced the opposite side of the building, so it was unlikely that they saw me. That was unless they had a link to the building's surveillance systems. I hoped they didn't, of course.

I slowed to a normal walk as I casually approached a parcel delivery guy from behind. He tapped the door access panel, one of the building residents answered; "Finally, God, I never thought my hoverboard would get here. It better be in pristine condition, it's from the beginning of the Third Era Miniaturisation Wave. That's over three hundred years ago, so it's more valuable than you are, a collectable," said a voice through the emitter.

"You gonna come up for it, or let me in?" the delivery man asked.

"Come on down." The double doors slid open and I walked in with the courier.

He glanced at me, then took a longer look. "Am I gonna get in trouble for letting you in?"

On a whim, I thought I'd try something and replied; "Freelance law enforcement. I'll leave you out of my report."

"Uh-huh. You're not here for Forty-Seven C by any chance?" he asked.

"No. Mine's on a different floor," I replied.

"Are you sure you don't have something on the bounty board for this guy? He's been hounding us for his crap for two weeks. A real prick."

"I'm about to have my hands full, sorry," I don't know why, but I took the brim of his hat in my fingertips and straightened it as I smiled and said; "You should make your delivery and take off. Fast."

The elevator doors opened and he stepped out, looking over

his shoulder for a moment. "Good luck, maybe I'll see you on the news."

"Hope not, but probably. Now, run," I said casually.

The elevator took me down five more floors. It wasn't hard to change how I was experiencing time then, but it was tricky. My digital processors were limited to thirty-three percent, if I let them ramp up higher, I'd start frying my bio-brain. That didn't mean I always felt like time was moving very quickly because my computer was running fast, in fact, my bio-brain was calling the shots, keeping me in a sort of mode where I was feeling time pass like any human would. That wasn't something I decided, it just felt natural. That was, until I knew I'd be facing a cyborg with military hardware installed. That's why I leaned into the speed built into my chest, and it felt so different.

Yeah, those emotions were still there, but I started to feel giddy, and as my surroundings seemed to slow down to about half speed because I was comprehending the data my sensors collected faster and my thought processes were speeding up. The exhilaration was new, and mentally preparing for the fight felt way too good. "Oh, this is dangerous."

My infrared sensors had a good look through the walls and I was able to pick my targets out. Yabrick had one of the Obrun pinned on the floor, while Zord was forcing the other on the table. He was holding something that looked like a hot blade, and I rushed through the door, trying to be quiet as I ran down the hall. I turned my audio receptors up until I could hear Zord. "I've gotta see how you're put together. I bet you've got bits I can sell." This was about to go very bad for the residents of Forty-Two E.

"No, please, we didn't do anything," squeaked the Obrun on the table.

There were a lot of reasons for me to stay disconnected from wireless networks, but I gave in, mentally calling Building Security and Medical Response using their wireless. I reported a home invasion and got an automated message. "I'm sorry, but our security staff are not equipped to address the issue you have specified. Please contact local law enforcement. We apologise for any inconvenience."

There was no answer from any Law Enforcement agency. I wasn't surprised.

This is one of those situations where you hope you won't need backup, but I really wanted to get medics on their way. The building had over a thousand residents even though it had only re-opened about six weeks ago. You'd think they'd have a support staff of some kind.

I adjusted my plan and set my communications system to notify the building that there was a fire on the fortieth to fiftieth floors. I made sure that it wouldn't be sent out right away, the timing had to be perfect. I scanned the hallway wall for a thin point and found one. Taking an electromagnetic pulse grenade in my hand, I ran down the corridor at full speed and then turned into the wall. I busted through to the waist, but my legs were still mostly in the hallway behind me. There was a solid structural bar at waist height that I thought I could break through, but I didn't even manage to bend it. I'd lost the element of surprise, so I got even less creative.

I let the fire alarm notification message transmit. The building picked it up and satisfied my need for noise with a shrill alarm. My desire for confusion was satisfied with brutally loud alarms and strobing red light that came from every corner.

Zord was leaning over one of the Obrun, holding a short sword that was glowing yellow. He really was about to cut her open. I made eye contact with him as I activated my grenade and tossed it inside. In the three seconds it took for it to go off,

I got through the hole I made. Zord deployed his helmet, which folded up from his shoulders to come together around his head.

"I could really use one of those," I said, imagining a jacket or light armour with a fold down helmet built into the collar.

I drew my Violator, set it to burst mode, and announced; "I'm enforcing a HATE order from Themis Security on behalf of the Tabrus Government. That is Hunt and Terminate. If you surrender, you will be taken to containment, otherwise, I've been ordered to execute Zord, Yabrik Skyl and Hovan Skyl."

Yabrik and Hovan were on the floor, twitching thanks to the electromagnetic pulse grenade. Unlike Zord, they hadn't sealed up in time to avoid pulse damage to their components. I was covered in skin that insulated me. Beneath that was a nice layer of protection that guided unwanted electricity around my body if it was too much for my systems to handle. Zord's blade cooled, the mechanism inside fried, and he straightened, dropping it onto the table.

The Obruns were fine - one on the floor under Yabrik while the other scrambled to get off the table. "My wall!" cried the one on the floor.

"They sent a nobody?" Zord looked insulted.

"Hey, I'm an up and comer! Didn't you hear about my work on the Darmen One? I took care of Ettin, you'll be easy." I fired three shots in a burst right at his helmet. Two hit, chipping pieces of metal off the slanted surface, leaving thermite behind that dug in and sparked violently as it burned deeper. One got through right away and he screamed, deactivating his helmet and digging the thermite out of the gorget protecting his neck.

With absolute certainty that Zord would be difficult to take down, I fired two more bursts. He raised a military-grade cybernetic arm with thick armour and blocked the triple shot that was meant for his head. The other three almost made their mark, impacting on his thick legs. I meant to get those into the narrow chink between that and his Vital Case. He let the forearm plate drop with a clatter so the thermite rounds wouldn't burn through to the equipment beneath.

Yabrik rolled off the Obrun he had pinned to the floor. The cyborg's legs weren't working. The furry Obrun ran to his mate and they rushed out of the apartment. Hovan started to reach for a weapon and I got moving across the living room, firing at him as I did. One round hit a metal plate covering half his face, and the second burst through his cheek as the third caught him in the mouth. These were shaped explosive thermite rounds. The one that hit the faceplate blasted it inward as the thermolytic part of the round started burning through the remaining metal. The other two exploded out the back of his head, a kill shot.

"Hovan!" Yabrick shouted as his brother slumped and convulsed.

Zord charged, flicking a pair of blades out from his arms. "Where did you put him?" He howled the question like a battle cry.

There was only time to fire one burst. One round hit his armoured thigh, the other two caught him in the chest. All of them burned and sparked, burning into his armour. He was twice my size in every direction, and most of his body had been replaced with cybernetics. Confirmed. This guy was real Street Metal, not some Cold Boy with second-hand industrial parts. I got out of his way at the last second, ducking a slash that cut through the wall behind me.

His other hand came too quickly, catching me by the head, pushing me half way to the floor as it tried to crush my skull. At first my head could take the punishment, but his thumb dented the metal with a loud creak and I became fully aware of one thing that changed everything going forward. This guy could end me.

I didn't allow the pain in, who would want that? It was a good thing he went after my head, but I'd just repaired most of what was in there, so it pissed me off just the same. He slashed at my right arm, trying to cut it off or force me to drop the Violator. I let the blade clash with my armour once. "Where did you put him?" he asked again, holding my head in one hand while he brought his blade around slowly, pointing them at my face.

Even though there was real damage, he was still underestimating me. My injury simulation systems were hard at work, showing splits in my skin, pumping blood over my face. Somehow this guy was still convinced that I was human even though he was putting enough pressure on my skull to dent a solid steel block. I fought for leverage as he pressed. "Who?" I let him think I was terrified as he bent down, bringing his face closer to mine.

He gripped my head harder, trying to control my body, to get me down onto the floor. Another creak filled my ears as my skull gave in a little more. The new balance I'd struck between digital processors and my bio-brain made me slower to anger, but when I got there it was a richer kind of fury. He spoke through clenched teeth then. "Bergio. Where did he hide his brain box?"

So, that was why they were watching Bergio's place! They thought someone would come along and collect Bergio's grey matter because it wasn't in his body. "You must have been disappointed when you didn't find his mind." I got my feet under me, pointed my pistol at his armpit, grabbed his wrist and let loose with two bursts that blasted through the joint and the internal components, leaving that limb hanging by wires.

Even after I stepped away, ripping those strands away from

his shoulder, the hand clung. I fired at the wrist, blasting the mechanisms that were keeping his fingers clamped on my head and was finally able to get it off. The dents in my skull were repaired immediately and the relief was amazing. That's when I turned and stared at him, holding his ruined arm like a club as my face was regenerated. "One arm down, one to go, then we'll get you off your feet."

"You're not taking me to the Pods," Zord said as he charged using a thruster hidden on his back.

To say I wasn't ready for that would be a gross understatement. His good shoulder collided with my chest and he bashed me into the transparisteel window at my back. My impact dampening systems - which were right under my collarbones - burned out mitigating the hit. I didn't have the material to rebuild them. Those are antigravity tech, expensive and custom because they're so miniaturised. They did save me from getting crushed outright, but my armour was absolutely trashed. My hip and chest protection were bent inward, and the arm joints were pushed out of place so I had to fight the suit to move.

It's times like those that I wished we were on one of the middle floors, where they used fortified glass. We would have gone right through, but the window bowed instead, nearly coming free of its frame. I got an idea and fired at the upper corner that was still holding the window pane in. As the thermite rounds burned, I looked him in the eye. "You wanna go down? We'll go down."

A flash of fear was all the reward I needed as I grabbed the collar of his armour and twisted my body out from under him. The transparisteel plate window came loose and he started to fall through it. I wanted to watch him drop over forty stories or, if that thruster hidden on his back got him in the air, blast him down. I had plenty of ammo left. I planted my foot on the floor and my boot gripped, saving me from going out the window with him.

He reached out and caught my arm, I shook it loose before he got a good hold, and then, in another burst of surprising speed, he caught my ankle. If I didn't get my other boot onto the floor just in time, we would have both gone down. His thruster spat flame for a second before I shot it. The fuel inside went off, filling the air with a concussive blast that nearly shook him loose.

It was time to end it. I fired at the top of his head, catching him with one round and then a second with my Violator. The first revealed that his skull was coated in metal beneath the flesh. The second dented it. My advantage disappeared as he grabbed the edge of the floor and yanked himself up and inside. With a furious cry, I grabbed him by the front collar of his Vital Case and brought him down onto the floor. "You want to go down, you want to come up, make up your mind!" I said, levelling my Violator at his head.

That was the last chance he had to surrender, but he blew it by trying to get to his feet. I switched my Violator back to burst mode and fired until my magazine was empty. His head busted wide open as his cybernetics drew him to his feet. By the time he was fully upright and balanced, there was nothing but burning, sparking gore above the shoulders. I stepped back and scanned him. There was no secondary brain in his Vital Case or anywhere else. The cybernetic systems were still except for a pair of gyros that worked to keep him on his feet.

Yabrik was crawling away. I reloaded my Violator and levelled it at him. "Why did you kill Bergio?"

He glanced at Zord's corpse as a piece of him tumbled down his chest. Then he looked at me. "Darman ordered it."

To my surprise, Hovan's voice came through a tiny speaker

built into his chest. "I told you we should have gotten the hell out of here as soon as we lost contact with Darmen One. This has always been a shit outfit."

His brain had been moved to his chest, probably nestled in a cybernetic life support system. If he wasn't such a murderous thug, I might have felt like he was a kindred spirit. His brother shook his head. "We don't know what happened. He said to stay here and watch for Bergio's people. He wanted to see who would come save him. Zord wanted to finish Bergio off because he knew how everything in his case was wired."

That made sense in a dark, paranoid way. If Bergio built Zord's vital case and everything inside, he would know his vulnerabilities. I scanned Zord again and when I was sure he wouldn't turn around and take my head off, I returned my attention to Hovan and Yabrik. "How do we finish this? Surrender or execution?"

"We were just following orders," Hovan said. "Zord was Darman's enforcer, would you go against him if you were us? We had no choice. Listen, we've got some plat stashed away, it's yours. Just don't drop us off with law. I don't want to serve time in a rehab pod. They'll re-case me in a basic, or put my vital organs in a host bag and hook me up to a full-dive connection until I forget there's anything else. Then I'll get out with a basic bi-frame if I'm lucky."

Okay, it's translation time. The Pod he's talking about is a Physical Operations Detention Device that manages an inmate's body. It's kinda like a coffin with indoor plumbing and it's supposed to have solid life support that keeps people in shape, free of so much of a bed sore while they serve days, months or years. I'd find out later that the prisoner is connected to a deep simulation that takes over all their sensations, so they forget that they're in a locked life support box, mostly. While they're in there they virtually live in a world that's specifically made to rehabilitate prisoners. How they do that is a whole other story, but that's the goal. They serve their time or check all the boxes for rehab and are set free. If it's a good prison and you have most of your body parts, then you come out healthier than you went in, just a little older. If it's not a good prison, then you may be missing a few things thanks to infection, have extreme atrophy or worse.

It's seriously bad for cyborgs regardless of where you go. Violent criminals have almost all their cybernetics removed and sold to help pay the prison's bills. That can include their Vital Case. When their heads and organs are moved out of their cases, they are often put into a much cheaper case, or they're transferred to a special life support unit that cares for their vitals and their heads or brains if there are no other organs. The inmate cannot do so much as flip their jailers the bird because they don't have limbs. They are connected to the simulation until they're all better in the brain and ready to rejoin society. When they get out, the best they get is a cheapo Vital Case along with a bi-frame, which is slang for a basic bipedal kit with arms and legs. You get a little head if your brain wasn't in the one you arrived with that's about the size of a human hand with very basic sensors and a cheap speaker so you can talk. The only good thing about the whole setup is that your new body is basically able.

About half of this information came along later, but even knowing that they'd be dropped into containment pods for years, I didn't have any sympathy for the brothers. According to the law, I could have killed them there and then. I'd get paid just the same.

"Oh, yeah, we can't get you any of the credits in the Corp

accounts, but whatever else, it's all yours. You can have my left arm, I mean, you name it," Yabrik added.

"I could shoot you both again so I don't have to carry you around," I said, pointing my Violator in their general directions. "Or, Pods."

"Son of a bitch, I hate rehab," Hovan said witheringly, his voice drifting up from the speaker in his chest.

"Maybe we could get an appeal or something?" Yabrik asked.

It only took me a second to check on that possibility and I nodded. "If you surrender you can appeal." I didn't feel good about that. There was video of them raiding and killing people in the wastes before they were mostly machine. They were criminals before they started replacing bits of themselves with metal.

"Problem is, someone could trigger us, make us dead if they know we're still around, you know? Darman pushes a button and we both go bang?" Yabrik said. "Unless we go back to the Darmen building."

My sensors didn't pick up any explosives or devices that could take them out, but I was tired of their yapping, so I decided to take drastic measures. "That probably won't work if your receivers are fried." This was the compromise, and it made me grin right there on the spot. I took an electromagnetic pulse grenade in each hand. "One for you, and you," I said as I lobbed them at the pair.

"No, no, no, no!" they shouted as they struggled to get away. When I say struggled, I mean their arms randomly twitched, having already been hit with a major pulse. When the grenades went off, they were twitching messes again. A scan revealed that Hovan's Vital Case couldn't keep his brain conscious anymore, so his grey matter was safely put into stasis. Yabrik's life support system stopped working altogether, and he was turning blue before it reset and started back up. I'd made a mess of them, but they survived.

I called Lat as I collected Bergio's arm. "All right, change of plans. I need a pickup. We've got two surrenders who need transportation. I'm sending you the coordinates now."

"Okay, I'm on my way," he replied.

"Fly well, don't rush and use the auto-lander," I said, cringing. I kinda wish I didn't say that, but I really didn't trust his flying.

"Don't worry, I can fly," he replied.

"You already broke something when you landed here. Be careful," I heard Mimi scold in the background.

"Weren't you in the bathroom?" Lat asked, surprised.

"I can't go in there, there's nowhere to squat. It's like a metal flower with holes in it. I don't even understand how it's a toilet!" Mimi squeaked, frustrated. There would probably be a mess to clean up when I boarded the ship, but I didn't get to listen to more of the conversation because the apartment's furry residents returned.

"You've ruined our home," said one Obrun with a thick accent.

Looking around, I could see that there was less damage than I thought. They had a few oval mattresses on the floor along with the table that was destroyed and a couple of small low tables. There was a holographic projector hanging from the ceiling, and I knew you could pick one of those up for a few hundred credits. The damage to the walls and floor would cost a few thousand, so I sent my sensor data of Zord's death to Themis, requesting a quick digital payment. "I'm sorry, these guys were wanted. I'll clear out as soon as my ship gets here."

"But..." the smaller Obrun said before turning to her mate and burying her face in his fur. Her crying came as little squeaks.

I got a message back from Themis along with a transaction

notice informing me that they'd transferred fifty-nine thousand and three credits to my Fi-Bank account. Most of it was for taking Zord out. The rest was from another anonymous party who wanted to reward me for dismantling the leadership of the Darmen Corporation. I didn't take the time to question it. Instead I looked at the Obrun. "I'm here enforcing a judgment, and the law says that I'm not responsible for the damage, but I know you were just caught in the crossfire," I took my glove off and raised my hand so they could see my stamp computer. "I want to make it right."

The female raised her head and slowly extended her arm. I tapped my computer to the band there, transferring five thousand, more than enough for them to pay for repairs and replace the electronics my grenades burned out. My stamp didn't work, but I used my real computer to make the transfer. My face had regenerated too, but that didn't stop the Obrun from reacting to the blood on my neck and cheek. "You are injured." The change in their attitude was remarkable after they saw how much money I gave them.

"Nah, I have a regenerative weave," I replied, describing a kind of cybernetic implant that a growing number of mercenaries were getting installed. "I'm okay."

She rushed off into the apartment and came back with a damp cloth. I let her wash the blood off as her mate said; "You really should wear a helmet."

"I keep forgetting it," I shrugged. My armour was trashed. The chest, back, right shoulder, and thigh plates were done and the electronics were fried. They didn't seem to pay much attention.

The Obrun were starting to talk about redecorating when Lat signalled me from the roof. "Well, that's my ride," I said sheepishly as I tied a restraint around Yabrik's ankles, then

Hovan's and dragged them behind me. "I've gotta get these two out of here."

"They're not dead?" one Obrun asked.

"They look dead," said the other, shocked.

"No, they're just shut down," I replied.

Almost through the door, I heard one of them shout after me. "What do we do with this?"

They were talking about Zord's corpse, which was still standing in their living room. "Call a scrapper. They'll give you something for it."

When I got to the ship, the ramp was already lowering. Two technicians in standard jumpsuits regarded me and the bodies I was dragging wide-eyed. "Uh, don't suppose you need refuelling?"

"Xetima? Sagum? Maybe coolant?" the other asked as though he'd done so a thousand times. He was staring at my captures.

"Two bounties. Fill 'er up though," I said, oddly proud and grinning as I pulled the bodies up the ramp.

"Are you Police?" one asked.

"Freelance Law Enforcement," I replied cheerily.

"Prettiest bounty hunter I've ever seen," one tech whispered.

"You did notice the two half-scrapped Street Metal 'borgs she was dragging, right?" the other said. "We really need to find you a date."

I closed the ramp, aware that they put a restraint on the ship so they could fill my tanks and hold us down while they waited to be paid. I had no idea how much fuel the Hinow-Sa had burned through, or if it needed other fluids. I should have checked, but I didn't bother since I first came aboard. Everything was full then.

Lat and Mimi weren't waiting for me in the back, so I looked around in the hold and found a few collapsed boxes exactly like the one I'd been put in earlier. After setting them up, I put one brother in each and sealed them up. After that, I looked for Lat and Mimi.

I was a little afraid of what I'd find, but I turned my sensors up, including the gain on my audio and snickered to myself at the scene on the other side of the bathroom's accordion door. Lat was gently holding Mimi up with her rear end pointed at the strange toilet, which looked like a narrow, curvy bowl with a hole in it surrounded by colourful metal petals that would make it awkward for any human or kitten to sit over or on while they did their business. "Like this? Is this okay?" Lat asked.

"Yeah, but don't look," Mimi was telling him. "I don't like to go if people are watching! I said don't look!"

"Okay, okay," Lat said, turning away, still holding her over the bowl.

I turned everything back down to normal levels and retreated. There would definitely be a little bonus for Lat later. That was also when I realised that I had a bad habit of rushing into rooms.

The small refill of our Sagum thruster fuel and coolant cost one hundred forty-nine credits and I paid it. The umbilical detached from the hull and I stood in front of the controls. Themis sent me the drop point for my bounties, but that would have to wait. I needed to visit Bergio's place.

CHAPTER FOURTEEN

Follow Up

When I set the Hinow-Sa down on Bergio's landing pad its cooling system suggested that I didn't take off for at least ten minutes. The ship wasn't made to fly in the atmosphere or areas over twenty-five degrees celsius for long. A quick lookup with the manufacturer - Sokie Industrial - revealed that this was their low end deep space light transport. Reviews rated it as a lemon. The chances of me selling it for anything other than scrap were dropping every time I looked it up. The workshop equipment in the hold would probably be worth more than the whole ship.

I sent cold air from the environmental conditioning systems through the main thrusters so they'd cool faster and made sure that it would stop after one minute. The engine cooldown time dropped to two minutes. I mentally checked on the Envoy, my other ship, and discovered that it had returned early after the security program I'd installed determined that it wasn't being followed. It also gathered data from several solar systems in our local cluster of solar systems. It was a relief to see that it was on its way to Tabrus from the outer solar system and I gave it instructions to land on the outskirts of New Zero. I didn't love the Envoy, it was more of a luxury craft than a fighting ship, but it sure beat the Hinow-Sa.

There were other messages waiting. A mercenary company called Shinefellow had been hired to clear out the Darmen One, and I was surprised to find a video message from the owner. I watched it at four times the regular speed. The image of a square jawed man with piercing blue eyes filled my head. He was grinning at me while he chewed gum. I could see three crewmen loading Ettin, or what was left of him, onto a hover cart. "Hey, Rogue. You left this joint in one hell of a state, we only had two short firefights before the whole boat was ours. Too bad you took out the bridge and the swank officer quarters got trashed, that makes the rest of the ship salvage, and that's not worth much here, so I'm gonna have to drag it to another system where they're buying scrap. Maybe right to the centre of the Ninety-Eight, to Haven. Their manufacturing spots are chewing more scrap down into their big fabs faster than anywhere else. There's a tip for ya. Here's another. When you take your bad day out on a gang of shitheads, call a few competing corporations first. We just got paid seven figures to finish what you started." he took a moment to chew his gum, staring into the holorecorder.

Before he continued, he looked over his shoulder at what was left of Ettin. He shook his head for a moment when he looked back at the recorder. "Now, I know all this might piss you off, and I saw what you did here. I mean, a few of the crew said you did this because a beef you had with one of the leaders. I'm going to have one of my guys transport what's left of her to the Rose System so we can cash that in. Thanks for that, I'll send you half. Oh, and her computer survived, and there's footage of your fight with her. Was I ever surprised when I saw what was under your skin. We're not uploading that anywhere, consider it a professional courtesy. Tell you what else I'll do. I'll deliver what's left of the ship you used to dock to the Darmen One wherever you want in the solar system. There's some nice loot in there, but my guys won't touch it. That is, if you agree not to contact any of the corporations that paid us to finish the Darmen off demanding a cut. So, you get back to me today so we can get squared."

When I took on Darmen One I wasn't thinking of making money, but I could see at a glance that the Shinefellow Company had found more crew members aboard who had bounties on them. So far they'd claimed thirteen. Some were worth four figures, and a few were worth five. It was irritating at first, but I quickly accepted that I didn't attack the Darmen One for money, and I'd take the whole thing as a lesson. What I learned there was to look enemies up before I leap in, and not to let revenge motivate me. As much as I didn't want to admit it, that's what really took me to that ship.

With a few thoughts directed at the Stellarnet, I reserved a larger hangar for the Envoy that would also accommodate what was left of my old ship and the Hinow-Sa, and then sent a response to Vasard, the owner of the Shinefellow Company. Taking Darmen One out of commission would be good for my reputation, but I wanted more than the credit because the thought of them making a fortune off of my work was almost as irritating as Vasard, who was or wasn't threatening to blackmail me. I couldn't be sure, but I wouldn't let it happen. "Thanks for getting in touch so I don't have to track you down myself. Your terms are all right, but you're going to cut me in for ten percent and give me Nera's recorder. If I see footage from it online, or you use it to suggest I'm some kind of android, I'll have to shut you up and destroy all the evidence. Get back to me fast, because I only have one errand to run before I settle into a hangar. I've got to deliver a couple Darmen Corp cyborgs to Themis. It's been a long day. I expect delivery of what's left of the Uwebo, its contents and my plat at Hangar Thirty-Seven in New Zero. You have two hours."

"What happened?" came Mimi's gasp from behind me.

I'd forgotten that I was still wearing my battered armour because I was so focused on what I was seeing online. News of the events aboard the Darmen One and the Darmen Corporation's building getting cleared out by another group of mercenaries was spreading fast. Their competition saw blood in the water and paid to have them wiped out completely. Liquidation sales were already scheduled for later that week.

Tearing my attention away from all that, I turned towards Mimi and Lat. "I'm all right, but I need a hand getting out of this suit."

"It looks like half the plates are about to fall off," Lat said, taking a more expert look at me. He cocked his head after looking at my face for a moment. I didn't have the empathic gift my sister did, but I could tell what he was thinking. With all that damage to my armour, how was my head in such good shape?

Instead of answering his question I yanked my reinforced gloves off and left them on a seat shaped like a flower. I knelt down in front of Mimi, who stared up with wide eyes. "I'm all right, they trashed my armour but didn't get through."

"There's a hole right there," Mimi said, looking at my side.

"Yeah, but I'm good. All patched up. Are you all right?" I asked her.

"I feel better now. Thank you for the tuna. I've never had it before," Mimi replied, shifting on her haunches a little.

"I bought it," Lat interjected.

"You're welcome. Everything else okay?" I asked.

"I don't like this place. It smells funny and I can't perch on the toilet," Mimi said, finishing in a whisper.

"My other ship is on the way. But for now, I need to cut myself out of this armour and investigate something." A text only response to my counteroffer came in, and I was a little surprised to read:

Three percent in platinum but only for clearing out the Darmen One. We keep bounties, contents and auction proceeds. Ettin isn't worth shit, we can't even auction him because you left him alive. We'll pay to ship him to the nearest Parvokib government. You still get what's left of your ship with everything we found inside - nice bike, by the way - and I'll toss you Nera's computer. No blackmail, don't worry. We can keep this friendly. Meet you at your High-Sec Hangar in New Zero. It'll take a bit, we've got to patch your ship for reentry.

Fairly certain that I could press him for a bigger cut, or to get a chunk of what he'd make from the bounties and auctions, I decided that I should let it go. The days of running around abandoned sections of Tabrus, tagging stuff for salvage and pulling platinum out of empty buildings were quickly coming to an end. I had to move on, get a real job, and if I was going to be doing bounty hunting and other mercenary work, then I might want a few friends in the field. If Vasard delivered on everything and I found the twenty-five thousand platinum in its case untouched in the Uwebo, then that would be a great start with him and his merry band of mercs.

My attention was drawn back to the present as Lat looked at me as though he could tell that my thoughts were far away. "So, I'm going to see the Envoy?"

"It's coming," I said, leading the way off the bridge.

Lat has steady hands and good listening skills. When I met him, he was questioning his objectives - to follow any and all instructions from Order of Eden Officers - and he barely think on his own. I told him he was free. He kind of adopted me as his new officer for five weeks. It was enough time for me to take him along for a bunch of scavenging trips and get him into the Haven Education Program, which was available to the general public. When I saw that he was devouring the courses like a dry sponge, I pointed him to the sciences, including some more social stuff. He did not do well with anything social.

That's why I was surprised when he started rebelling against me. When I said something was white, he would argue that it was black. At first I was irritated, even insulted. Then I clued in. Somehow Lat was learning that he didn't have to have an officer giving him orders. He could pick his own course and follow it. When he left a few days later, I made sure he knew he would always be welcome back. I don't regret that in the least, but seeing him return to the Quarry, admitting that he'd run into trouble in the wastes was another surprise. I'm not disappointed that he had to come back, but I wish he'd take the pill filled with nanobots that would remove the Framework system from his body, really freeing him from the Order.

As Mimi watched him use a rotary cutter to grind through the braces at the back of my armour with steady hands, I was thinking about our history. Mimi watched from where she sat atop a worktable. If I got into bounty hunting things would change. "A group of mercs are going to be delivering what's left of my old ship to a hangar I rented in New Zero. It looks like we'll be in better shape by the end of the day."

"Oh?" Mimi asked with interest. She thought I was talking to her, so I kept it up.

I was sure Lat was listening just as attentively. "There's something else. I'm going to use the Themis Boards to find jobs. The three bounties I picked up are worth fifty-k each."

"Platinum?" Lat asked as he got through the last brace on the back of my armour and moved on to my waist.

"About thirty thousand platinum altogether," I replied.

"Your armour isn't worth repairing. Replacing it will cost two or three thousand platinum, but you should get a better suit. That'll cost a lot more," Lat explained. "Did you lose anything else?"

It was a little annoying to have my work measured simply by comparing the cost to the reward, especially by someone who didn't have the kind of information I did. "I'm making money here, don't worry."

"The damage is significant. Even your shirt got cut up. You shouldn't have gone alone," Lat said flatly.

"I handled it. Maybe I made a few mistakes, but they weren't serious enough to get me slagged. I didn't need help this time," I replied, looking over my shoulder.

Lat finally got through the armour brace at my waist and I was able to pull the pieces apart enough to push them down over my leggings as I listened to his response. "I still think I should have gone with you."

"Have you ever gone up against a cyborg with military hardware?" I asked, turning towards him.

"No. I know how to fight machines though. They're the

same," he replied, putting the cutter back on the hook where he found it.

Mimi almost made me laugh when I noticed her rolling her eyes at Lat. Even she knew that wasn't true. "Cyborgs and machines, even ones driven by complex AI, are different. One is more unpredictable; personality is a factor. The other is more logical, and an AI can ignore or account for all kinds of things that a biological being can't. A machine can turn its feelings off sometimes, or access new data that will make it behave differently. There's more to it, but you get what I'm saying. Training to deal with pure machines doesn't get you ready for the kind of crap I had to deal with today." I almost lost my patience as he started picking up pieces of my torso armour. I couldn't say he accepted half of what I said.

"I understand," he replied. Lat nodded at the pieces of armour in his hands. "Recycler?"

"If it'll handle it," I replied. I was about to ask him to join my crew earlier, but it didn't feel like the right time anymore. I regarded Mimi then, who was looking at something on the floor. "I have something to check out. There won't be trouble, and I should only be gone for a few minutes. Half an hour, tops."

"Okay," Mimi replied.

It was nice to see that she wasn't giving me the cold shoulder anymore, even though I was sure she wasn't totally over Bergio. If he was still alive somehow, I wanted to make sure before I got her hopes up. "The recycler won't process your armour," Lat said as he dropped the plates in a bin then pushed it under the workbench. "I'm going with you."

"No, you're watching the ship," I said, pointing down at Mimi.

"I saw that," Mimi said as she brushed up against his ankle.

"Okay. Have you done an inventory?" he asked.

"No, good idea," I replied.

After checking, reloading and holstering my Violator, I opened the aft ramp and shouldered the pack I'd put Bergio's arm in. Okay, so at this point I think it's fair to mention that I have a bad habit of not taking what's on the other side of a door seriously. It would get me into trouble. As soon as I started down the ramp, Mimi shouted; "Home! You took me home!" and ran past me.

"Hey, I told you to stay on the ship!" I called after her.

"No, you told him to stay, you told me you'd only be gone for a few minutes," Mimi called back.

I actually remembered what I said or didn't say as soon as she started talking, but she slowed down enough for me to pick her up without breaking into a run. "Okay, you're with me. If I cover your eyes it's because I don't want you to see something. I'm protecting you."

"Okay. If I bite your hand, it's because I don't need protecting and you should let me look around my own house," Mimi said.

"Bergio gave you to her. She's your master now," Lat said as he caught up.

I regarded him with an upraised eyebrow.

"What? If she's not staying on the ship, I'm not staying," he replied with a shrug.

Shaking my head, I continued down the bridge leading to Bergio's door. I held Mimi gently, but firmly, giving her a scratch behind the ear. "A little higher," she whispered, tilting her head so my finger hit the right spot.

The doors opened, and I felt her tense. I didn't know much about cats back then, so I thought I had a good hold on her. How wrong I was. She got free with a quick wriggle. I could have tightened my grip, caught Mimi before she hit the floor, but there was a chance I'd hurt her, so I let her go.

We still ran after her, and she found Bergio's head under a worktable. "Noooooooo," she yowled, rubbing up against his face.

With care, I picked her up and she hissed in my arms. "You shouldn't have left him! This is your fault!"

"Don't blame her," came Bergio's voice from a small hovering disk as it slipped out of his desk from a hidden slot. It hovered in front of us. A hologram followed, life-sized and rendered in pretty good quality. "I knew dealing with the Darmen Gang would eventually bring me to an abrupt end. None of those psychotic waste landers were going to let me live for too long while I knew exactly how they were wired."

"I can't smell him, is he real?" Mimi asked, shifting around and using my arm as a perch.

"I think so," I replied.

"I'm so lucky for you, Mimi," Bergio said, bending down towards her. A nearly inaudible hiss came from the disc as a thin spray was sent up from it.

"It is him!" she said, leaning towards his image so far that I had to hold her hind legs so she didn't fall.

"You've been around for nearly a year while I've been working on those cyborgs, so I know you'll understand when I tell you that the body you knew never had my brain in it. The bravest, craziest and oldest cyborgs never leave it where nature put it. I'm not crazy and I usually don't have to be brave, but I am older than your young mind can understand. An explorer. Someone who has had many lives, experiencing them through different bodies. I stay for a while, and then it's time to move on. I didn't expect to survive the Fourth Fall, but I did, and I got reckless. I was curious about a gang that was trying to transition into a corporation, so this is my fault. Now it's time for me to start over somewhere else."

"Don't go. Don't leave me with her. She has a very strange toilet," Mimi whispered to him urgently.

He laughed and replied; "I made you to be an extraordinarily intelligent Kawaii Kitten. You're also stronger, a little faster, have a great deal of curiosity. I even managed to get your shedding under control. Rogue is the perfect owner for you. She will guard you with her life and show you things I could scarcely imagine. Well, maybe I could, but I've been around a bit more than most. Besides, I'm moving on. It's time. My mind never left the jump ship I arrived here in. It's building a new body for me right now. You need to find a new favourite person, and I think Rogue may be the one. I know more about her than she thinks, having tracked her since she arrived on Tabrus. She's one of the more morally centred people on this planet, from what I've seen, and I've tracked thousands of wasteland scavengers."

Okay, so I usually don't like it when people know more than I do, but I didn't suspect that Bergio had any nefarious intentions. If anything, I had a growing list of questions for him. I was also kind of at a loss for words, since I didn't know where to start. "Thanks. Are a lot of people watching the wastes?"

"There are a few who managed to hide and maintain connections to satellites and active surveillance systems in the abandoned places," Bergio replied. "Look to heads of industry, and political fixers, you'll find some of them." He looked at my bag then and asked; "Is that my arm?"

"Yes," I replied.

"Keep it, or sell it," he said. "It'll fetch a good price. Then stop dealing with combat cyborgs unless you must."

"That's a good idea," I agreed, tired of them already. "Are you sure about the arm, though?"

"Do what you like with it. My next body won't be a cyborg, except for the neural connection." He looked down to Mimi then. "I'll miss you, Mimi. Well, until I have children. I think I'll have a family during the next go. It's been about a century." Mimi's collar flashed and a message scrolled across it that said;

Congratulations, Rogue! You are now Mimi's Special Person! Please take good care of her. Instructions have been sent to your Ident Number.

The sounds of doors opening and motors running drifted up from below. The roar of a rocket engine firing preceded the appearance of an old, long ship with a thick hull that was eleven metres long. From the limited information I could find, it was probably six hundred years old, and mostly hull. There were upgrades since its construction, judging from the way it skipped across the sky, accelerating faster than most star fighters.

"Are you sure about her? She's keeping someone in the closet," Mimi asked Bergio's hologram.

"I'm sure she has her reasons, Mimi. Rogue has a more complicated life than we did. It's time for you to go with someone who has adventures since you outgrew my apartment months ago. Most importantly, I can tell she likes you in a way I never did. To me, you were an ongoing and very successful experiment. To her, you can be a companion who is welcome to steal all her attention more often than you could ever capture mine."

Mimi looked up at me before returning her attention to Bergio's hologram, which was starting to flicker. "You know, I was going to say something about you being a little too chilly."

"You mentioned it often," Bergio laughed. "Do as Rogue says, she's your master now."

"We'll see," Mimi said, already turning so she could lay along my chest as she turned her head to see Bergio.

He looked at me again and spoke more hurriedly. "I'm about

to go out of range. That means that all the data stored in my apartment, including any information about you or your visits, will be deleted when my drives self-destruct. Don't worry, there won't be explosions or fire, my storage will simply liquefy. My insurance policy will be activated. A team will respond. They will clean the apartment and then sell it and everything inside so the value of my possessions can be donated to various causes that I've already selected. There won't be anything here for you or Mimi once I've gone."

"I understand," I said, stopping myself from asking any of the questions on my mind.

"Thank you for adopting Mimi, and for taking care of those three across the way. They got what they had coming to them, thanks to you," Bergio said, sounding more satisfied than I expected.

"I thought you were a pacifist?" I asked.

"Usually, but then, being a pacifist is like being a vegetarian. You either are one, or you're enjoying a chicken wrap. I suppose, when it all comes down to it, my morals boil down to one thing. All that really matters is your grey matter and your escape plan. Farewell," he said as his hologram flickered.

"Goodbye Bergio, thank you," Mimi said in a sing-song tone.

"Oh, one more thing," Bergio said as his disk moved to Lat so his hologram was standing nose-to-nose with him. "Take your medicine before you catch one of the Order's transmissions and disappear. They're turning units like you into assassins, soldier boy."

The hologram disappeared, momentarily replaced with another that read; SIGNAL LOST for a moment before the disc deactivated and fell. I picked it up and put it in my pocket. Lat had a sour look on his face as I passed him. I didn't know what to say about Bergio's instructions, so I settled on what I thought should come next. "I guess we're leaving."

"What do you think he meant? Is the Order transmitting regeneration patterns that turn soldiers into something else?" Lat asked as he followed.

"That's almost exactly what he said, only he told you it would be assassins," Mimi said. "I don't know what he meant about medicine, but if it'll stop that, maybe you should take it? Oh, and get your hearing checked too. That was all pretty easy to understand."

"My hearing is perfect," Lat said.

"So, can I have a bed?" Mimi asked as she settled into my arms.

"Sure, it should be in your bag," I replied.

"That's just a blanket. Bergio thought it was a bed, but it really wasn't. I mean a bed. With a cushion."

"Sure, I'll set something up on the Envoy," I replied, stroking her soft fur.

Mimi gasped and asked; "Does it have a normal toilet? I'm trained to use the kind humans do, or a little one."

"Yes, it'll have normal plumbing," I replied.

"Tell me the Envoy has a shower," Lat said peevishly. "I tried the hygiene closet in the Hinow-Sa and I lasted ten seconds. There are arms that poke, scrape and pick, I don't recommend it."

"I can't wait to trade that ship in for scrap," I sighed.

If I'm being honest, I still feel guilty about getting Bergio involved. Somehow he saw the destruction of his body as a natural end point to a life that was dedicated to helping people, even if some of them were scumbags. If it wasn't for me, he would still be in his apartment, living with Mimi, fixing everyone who he could and doing research on whatever he liked.

The beginning of his end was forced, as far as I was concerned, and I was starting to feel like my pride caused a lot of problems. I didn't have to go after Nera, I could have let it go after causing all kinds of damage to Darmen Corp during my escape. I thought it was important to take the whole thing as a lesson that could help me put things into perspective so I wouldn't get carried away again. It didn't take the first time around.

CHAPTER FIFTEEN

Settling the Closet Dweller Problem

Mimi was eager to see where we were going, so keeping her off the control console was a challenge. While I guided the Hinow-Sa to Hangar Thirty-Seven her back foot came down on the Inertial Dampener Reset button and I had to be extra careful since everything inside the ship would be under the full influence of gravitational forces while we landed. "Lat, can you pick her up and hold her so she can see outside?"

"But, buttons. I want the buttons," Mimi whined as he did so with surprising care, supporting her feet with one hand and holding her steady with the other.

"Sorry, it's not safe," I explained, looking up from my instruments. New Zero's port was so large that it overwhelmed an entire Stonelands Valley. The original colonists quickly ran out of names for all the different features on the planet, and you could tell. There's a river called Jennifer. Seriously, Jennifer River.

Maybe there's a love story behind that, but I think the early settlers started naming things after each other while they were mapping the planet out. It doesn't matter much now though, because Jennifer River is pretty much forgotten. It runs under New Zero, completely out of sight.

Few streets are visible from above New Zero's Port. The ground is covered by old metal buildings and thick armour. A few towers stand out with hardened metal fins fanning out between the floors. I passed one that was still damaged from a collision as Navnet took control of the Hinow-Sa. That's what the fins were for, to give ships something to hit before they struck the outer walls of the buildings, but they also made the skyline of The Stonelands Districts of New Zero look jagged and sinister.

The disintegration cannons below didn't help with that. Most of them were active again, their large barrels sweeping the sky. They were the last point of defence against ships that came down too fast or anything that wanted to bomb the city. There were star fighters on patrol higher up, out of sight. You could see the shimmer of energy shields around some buildings, especially the newer ones. The oldest sections of the massive hangar city were easy to pick out since the buildings there used metres of hardened material. They were built before the latest generations of miniaturisation, before energy barrier shields were common. Ships like the First Light and stations like Freeground shared some of the building philosophies, where layered materials passively protected them from high radiation and attack. Freeground ships were late to the miniaturisation party, with so much mass that the ship classification system was totally different from the modern one. The buildings made with the old methods looked monolithic, ancient, invincible, even with thick transparent metal windows.

There could be millions of people living and working beneath us in those bunker like buildings, and towers but most of New Zero's port was unoccupied. I would have loved to buy a hangar there, especially an armoured one, but the Tabrus Government was charging three million credits for the size I wanted, and I wasn't looking at anything huge or unreasonable. That, and you had to clear it yourself and provide your own security.

I looked at the circular landing pits as we passed over them, the exact type I wanted with reinforced iris style doors. The ship turned towards a tall, fat tower with hangar doors facing every direction. It was hollow, and we slowly flew above it, joining a pattern that brought us down. I remember looking at the cost of the building a while ago, shortly after I arrived, and saw that it cost nine billion credits.

Themis bought it. The entire thing. They were already leasing hangars, and there were even apartments that were on the expensive side. There was definitely an appeal to parking your ship and living in a high security building like that. They even advertised discounts on repair services for residents, but I wasn't exactly earning the kind of plat I needed to live there. The Themis Complex wasn't where we were staying, it was where we would be dropping my bounties off.

Floor after floor went by as we descended into the middle of the building, slowly passing internal hangar doors and windows. There was little sign of life and I assumed that it was mostly empty, like the rest of New Zero's Port City. The navigation system showed that ships above and below us were finding their way into hangars, and we could see them landing as we continued down.

Then we saw something at about ground level that I didn't expect: A holographic Spectral Dynamics banner and several levels of clear metal walls all around us. Through them we saw a circular assembly line where hulls that varied between thirty-five and fifty metres in length were having thrusters, turrets, sensors, antenna and all kinds of other external parts installed. Workers hung along the sides on harnesses, walked around in exosuits that allowed them to carry heavy hardware into and around the ships as industrial robot arms drew sections of the hull aside. The banner followed us down and it started to play an advert.

In the hologram there was a thin, broad ship with a large collection of antennae and dishes on the front, a cockpit behind and above, with one large main thruster. We were treated to an idyllic vision of it flying towards a green-blue planet. As the announcer spoke in a powerful baritone, it continued on, passing into an atmosphere, over craggy mountains and fields of giant crystals. "Spectral Dynamics is proud to introduce a new age in space flight with a line of customisable Clippers."

"Look, they're putting a nice room into that one," Mimi said as we passed a bay where a living module was being pushed into the back of one of the ships by a pair of arms. It was complete with a sofa, counters, a food fabricator and cupboards built into its bulkhead.

"Quiet, I want to hear the man," Lat said.

"Oh, sorry," Mimi replied.

The announcer went on as the holographic ship caught up with an ice comet, the light reflecting off of its white-blue tail illuminating its hull. Its configuration changed from a single thruster model with a large sensor kit in the front to one with three thrusters in the back and an observation bubble on its nose. The cockpit moved up to the front of the ship too, offset from the middle. "With twenty-two exterior modification kits and fifty-five internal modules available for installation, your Clipper can be anything you like, help you do anything you need to do. Want to see the sights? With luxury passenger modules and the Stargazing exterior modification kit, your clipper can observe the wonders of the galaxy. Thanks to its manageable size, you can get close enough to see everything you like with the naked eye. With engineering sockets for many classes of jump and wormhole drives, you can even get there faster. Future support for Quad Drives is included, but compatibility is not guaranteed." As the announcer finished, the ship passed into a wormhole and changed again. The bubble was replaced with a tractor beam and grapple system in the front. Layers of thick hull plating covered the ship, gun and missile turrets were added.

I stood straighter, listening closely. "The Spectral Dynamics Clipper Law variant includes a next generation tractor beam with an artificial mass generator, can use a variety of turrets, emitters capable of supporting an interdiction system, enhanced hull plating, defensive energy shielding, a brute force airlock, and the stasis brig you'll need to contain the most hardened criminals. Military, law enforcement and bounty hunter consultants worked to make sure this is the best small hunting ship in space."

The holographic ship's weapons sent blasts of light at an imaginary foe as pulse cannon fire was deflected by its shields. Then, as the Clipper entered a wormhole and we watched it accelerate, the announcer finished his pitch. "Versatility, power, speed, comfort. The spirit of freedom. The Spectral Dynamics Clipper."

We passed out of its range. "You can't dig that out of the dirt," I muttered.

"We need one," Lat said.

"As long as there's room for my bed," Mimi said, nodding at him. "Maybe I could get one of those observation bubble things too."

I checked the crappy camera pointing down from the keel of the Hinow-Sa and saw that two heavy doors were parting for us. As we passed between them I was surprised to see that they were five metres thick. I looked for details on where we were going. Themis had their processing and temporary holding area underground in a converted prison. This is where my captures would be stripped of their legs and arms. Something came to mind then, and I turned away from the controls after making sure that Navnet was still firmly in control. "Where are you going?" Lat asked as I rushed out of the cockpit.

"To check on someone," I replied, opening the closet. Normally I wasn't forgetful. In fact, it seemed almost impossible to forget things before I began to try to balance my bio-brain with my digi-brain. I started to consider that using my synthetic grey matter all the time was making me more human, but that might come with a little forgetfulness along with a big emotional spectrum.

"Oh, hey, how's it goin?" asked Synchron, looking up at me with drowsy eyes.

I didn't need my sensors to see that he was in need of a nourishment pack, which Ettin kept several kilograms of. I rushed into the weirdo's quarters, where there was a nest like bed hanging from the ceiling and an upright support frame against one wall. Grabbing a two litre bag of the thick brown solution, I went back to the closet. "I'm sorry, I didn't mean to keep you in there for so long. Your systems are slowing your metabolism so they can keep you alive longer."

"Hey, I thought there was something going on with my metaboo, what's that?" he asked, looking at the large bag.

As I offered him the spout I replied; "It's Ettin's nutrient... stuff. I scanned it, it'll give you everything you need."

"That doesn't look like the emergency packs I use. Too...

brown." With hesitation he put his lips on the spout and I twisted the knob, letting some of the thick liquid out. He struggled with it a little and finally swallowed, his damaged arm flailing momentarily. After he'd had a few mouthfuls, I turned the spigot off and gave him a break. "God, I don't know whether to drink or chew, and it tastes like berries and chrome polish."

I'm not proud of any part of this, but I checked his criminal record with Themis and all the other organisations in range only to find that not only was Synchron's record clean, but I'd illegally confined him. If I wanted to be on the right side of the Bounty Boards, I had to be professional. That meant putting my feelings about Synchron screwing Bergio aside. Reporting nothing to anyone, I turned my attention back to him. "Uh, I'm really sorry. Do you want more?"

He shook his head. "Feeling better now. You forgot about me, huh?"

"Yeah. You were safe the whole time though," I replied.

"We're setting down," Lat shouted from the cockpit.

Mimi walked over to the closet and peered in, drawing Synchron's attention. "Oh, hey, cutie. I'd give you a scratch, but I'm unarmed."

"He's funny, can we keep him?" Mimi asked me.

"Only if you help me get some limbs. I've got a whole human analog set back at my place. We can just drop back there and I'll forget you kept me in a closet," Synchron said.

"I'll get you there. Until then, Lat will take care of you," I said as Lat joined us.

Synchron looked up at him for a moment then turned towards me and said; "I'd rather sit in the closet with a bag of mush. I mean, if it'll only be a couple hours."

"See? He's fine. I can go with you so I can see the bounty turn-in," Lat said, hanging the bag on a hook and lowering it.

"Wait, where are we?" Synchron asked.

"The Themis Complex. I'm turning in the Skyl brothers," I replied.

"Wasn't there a third target?" Lat asked.

"Zord. I already got paid for that one because no one wanted the body, just proof of death," I replied.

Synchron's eyes widened as I spoke. "You killed Zord and captured his insane pet assholes? I'll wait until you're all done with your turn-in, you can take a little time to do some shopping, sight-seeing, whatever. Just, you know, whenever you get around to dropping me off, that'll be fine. Take your time, leave me in the closet if you want, I'll be okay."

"You are intimidated by her," Lat laughed.

"I don't get your sense of humour," Mimi said as she watched him.

"Listen, you're not my captive, I was pissed at you before because you burned Bergio, but..."

"He whaaaaat?" asked Mimi, adding a hiss in his direction.

"Yeah, he's the one who told the Darmen that I'd gone to see Bergio," I explained to Mimi.

Mimi, who was in Lat's hands, stretched towards Synchron's face as she hissed hatefully and swept at him with her claws. "I didn't know!" he cried, cringing.

"Maybe we should keep you so she has something to scratch," Lat said, not pulling Mimi away, but providing a platform for her.

"Close the door!" Synchron said as he tried to shrink away from the cat.

"They tore him apart!" Mimi hissed as she struggled to get closer.

"Oh, you're cutting me," Lat told her as he held her with both hands.

She got one good slash in on Synchron, drawing four deep red lines down his cheek. "Whoa, this won't change anything," I said as I took her in my hands. She fought me for a moment, digging claws into my fingers. I held her close to my chest then. "Bergio's moved on," I whispered to her.

That calmed her down, but she turned in my hands and looked at Synchron. "Leave him in the closet. I don't wanna see him."

"Yeah, close the door, I'll be good in here until I get a drop off, okay?" Synchron agreed. He was terrified of our little Mimi, and I couldn't blame him. Sure, it would take her a while to scratch him to death, but that was part of the nightmare.

Lat made sure that the nutrient bag was hanging low enough for his mouth to reach it and closed the door as I said; "I'll get you home today."

"Whatever, just, you know, in one piece. Well, without the extra cuts," he replied.

I led the way back into the hold then whispered at Mimi and Lat. "Okay, that could be a problem. If he reports me for keeping him in a closet for most of a day, I could be charged with unlawful confinement. We need to get him back home as soon as we're done here and he'll have to either be too grateful or terrified to report me."

"I can scare him," Mimi said with relish.

"Why don't we put him in the floating bed? There's an entertainment thing in there, a projector," Lat said.

I peeked past him through the door to Ettin's quarters. He was right, a torso would nestle in well on that soft hammock like bed, and there were holographic emitters installed along the ceiling. That didn't take care of the biggest problem though. I had to get him home, but wait, did it really have to be me? "I have an idea," I said, turning to one of the computer consoles in the workshop.

I checked the local jobber boards and found the transportation section. There was a subsection for injured or medically dependent passengers with over ninety people running city transportation available in New Zero. I found an ambulance service who claimed to have 'all clearances. Will pick up anywhere and drop off in any city.' "Okay, never mind all this back and forth. I'm going to have him picked up." I sent my location along with Synchron's physical state and discovered that they had clearance with Themis to enter their containment area. After transferring a little over fifteen hundred credits, which was a hefty fee for a ride, they dispatched an ambulance. "Done. They'll be here in eighteen minutes."

"That is fast," Lat said, impressed

"But..." Mimi said, disappointed. "He'll just gets to go home?"

I put her on a worktable and looked into her eyes. "Okay. It's up to you. Leave him in the closet or get him out of our hair. I could be in trouble if we keep him longer though."

Mimi paced back and forth for a few moments and then sat down. "Okay, if it'll keep you out of trouble, he should go."

"Yes, Ma'am," I replied, turning towards the fabricator behind me. I needed to replace the stamp communicator on the back of my hand, and I hoped there was something I could use in the workshop. After rooting around in a set of little drawers beside it, I found a computer module, a single chip system with everything I'd need for the time being. I fed it into the machine and programmed it to install it into a bracer with a basic holo-projector, sensor set, and recording systems. It started printing.

"What? Just like that? You're just gonna do what I say?" Mimi asked, shocked.

When I turned around, she was wide-eyed. "It's pretty easy when we agree."

"Would you have left him in the closet if I told you to keep him there?" Mimi asked.

"Sure, I left it up to you," I replied.

"Bergio never asked me what I wanted," she said, her tail twitching as she considered the implications.

"She doesn't always let me do what I want either. Don't get used to it," Lat said.

"Oh, so there are limits. Interesting," Mimi said.

While they were talking I performed a scan of the ship using my internal sensors. I reviewed the results, doing a quick inventory of what was inside. "Okay, we're not keeping anything here. It's all going to scrappers," I said with a sigh.

"We haven't done an inventory," Lat said.

"I scanned the ship. This thing is filled with cybernetic parts that aren't made for any species that hangs out in the solar system and the ship isn't exactly top of the line. Even the workshop isn't anything special. It's pretty complete, but I'd spend mid five figures on upgrades if I kept it."

"I'm sure someone could use a ship like this though," Lat said.

"I don't want to wait around for a buyer who plans on adapting it for normal bipeds. It's scrap. I'll sell it as bulk mass if I have to."

"There really isn't anything valuable aboard?" Mimi asked, looking around. "Look at all that stuff hanging on the walls."

"They're tools. We can take them with us," Lat said.

"Even those aren't anything worth getting excited about. We should grab them because it's a pretty new set though, it's a good idea," I replied.

I pulled the burned out stamp computer off the back of my

hand and checked on my new, only slightly better, bracer. It was only sixty-three percent complete. I could see several small extruders and fusers working away.

"Are you leaving me behind?" Lat asked.

The phrasing caught me by surprise. "Well, I can bring you back to the Quarry, or you could move over to the Envoy. I could use your help delivering those guys," I said, nodding at the two white oblong boxes in the corner.

"So, I'm not part of your crew?" Lat said in his flat tone. He was difficult to read when he was gathering information.

"Do you want to be?" I asked.

Mimi was listening closely, looking at us in turn as we discussed it. "I do, but I want to do more. I'm a soldier. I have training."

"I know, and I'll put you to work, but I need you to keep training so you can help maintain a ship, learn the laws wherever we go, and figure things out on your own. I can help, but you have to keep it up."

"I will," Lat replied. "I enjoy the training."

"You'll have to get rid of the Framework system. I don't want to shoot you but I will if you start to turn into an order grunt. Listen, taking that pill really is like going to sleep and waking up without it. Those nanobots were developed to get rid of the Framework non-lethally by good people, smart people."

"Bergio used to use gas to put me to sleep after telling me that I'd wake up smarter. It's true, it always worked," Mimi told him, nodding. "Well, I think it worked. Do we all truly know how intelligent we are? Even objective tests aren't accurate all the time. Anyway, Bergio said it worked every time he did it, so I think you should do whatever she's saying."

That was something I would ask more about later, but I was just glad that she was trying to help at the moment. Lat looked down at the grey pill hanging in a case from his chain and then back up at me. "Have you seen it happen?"

"Several times. I've never seen it fail and people always come out remembering everything," I replied, continuing more softly then. "I want you to join my crew. I don't want the Order to wipe you out the first time you take that off." I glanced at the transmission blocker partially hidden in his hair.

"All right. As soon as we find a safe place for me to lie down," he replied. "You have to call someone on that list back though."

That got my hackles up, but I couldn't tell you why. "You're the one who wants to join my crew, you don't get to..."

"You've never said anything about any of those people that makes me think they want to hurt you. Why not see what they want to say? Maybe they can help? It's more important now because it won't just be you, it'll be us." Lat surprised me when he glanced at Mimi. I think he adopted her faster than I did. Giving her to a safer home would have broken all three of our hearts, so I was pretty sure I was looking at my crew of two.

The unease that brought at being responsible for them didn't measure up to the happiness ending my lonely days brought. The condition Lat proposed was a problem though. The people on the list he was talking about could help. I had a feeling that I could ask for a lot and they'd send me hardware or data that would make my life a lot easier. They may even be able to solve the insulation problem in my chest, but they weren't my people.

The list of contacts, messages and ignored calls was a compilation of Alice's people, and I wasn't ready to talk to any of them. I still considered it though. There was one that made me squirm less than the others, so I nodded. "All right. Don't expect them to start sending military tech and treasure maps though."

"That's not the point. When I moved into the Quarry the first time you told me that trustworthy people were rare, and you shouldn't ignore them. I didn't go through the messages, but some of them have summaries everyone can see. They want to help, I think. Maybe you can trust some of them?" Lat finished with a shrug.

Normally I'm not a fan of having my own words brought up, but it was reassuring to hear that something I told him a while ago stuck. It was surprising because he was completely self-centred when I met him back then. It irked me a little too because I thought I was doing pretty well in the self-improvement category, but I guess it wasn't showing yet. "I get your point. So you take that pill and I'll give someone who's been trying to reach me a call."

"A call and a conversation," Lat added.

"Right. Leaving a message doesn't count," I agreed.

"It has to last at least ten minutes," Lat said.

"Don't push it."

He held his hands up. "All right."

"So, you're a crew member. We're a crew," I said letting it sink in. The fabricator beeped. I opened the door and took my new bracer. It felt familiar as I closed it around my wrist, checking the matte black surface for burrs or other defects. The simple display lit up and indicated that it was booting for the first time. "Looks good."

After I tapped my Ident onto the back of the hand it did a cursory biometric scan I uploaded the rest of my day-to-day account access stuff to it from the computer built into my chest. To Lat, it looked like I downloaded that stuff using the public connection offered by Themis, but that was the last thing I linked to after all my security software was installed.

A loud chirp on the ship's intercom made everyone jump, including me. There were three workers at the back with a gurney. I pressed a button on the console and the ramp lowered.

"Permission to come aboard? We're here to pick up Synchron," one of the Emergency Medical Technicians said, raising his helmet's visor.

"This way," I said, leading them to the closet.

"Dangerous?" the one in heavy plate armour asked as I swept the door aside.

"Oh, hey fellas, is that my ride?" Synchron said, looking at the gurney with surprise.

"He's not dangerous. We kept him there because the ship ran into some trouble," I explained.

"Smart. This closet has its own emergency life support," one of the Emergency Medical Technicians said. "All right, Synchron, I'm Vince, that's my partner Corey, and the security officer over there is Brendan. We'll make sure you get where you're going in good shape, and he'll take care of any trouble along the way. Ready to go home?"

"Absolutely," Synchron said.

"All right, I'm connecting to your vital case here so we can see what's going on." He plugged a line into Synchron's chest and watched the indicators on a Flexi sheet display come to life. "You're all right, recovering from a short period of malnourishment, but all good. Is it okay if we put you on the gurney where you can be secure?"

"Go ahead, thanks," Synchron said as he regarded me with a stunned expression. "Can't believe you called the pros."

"I'm paying for it too. I want to make sure you get home safe," I replied. I know, he screwed Bergio over. Even after he saved me from some serious damage, sacrificing his legs, one and a half arms and spending the rest of the day in the closet, I still didn't feel like everything balanced out. Watching the EMT's take care of him so well made me feel better about my chances at avoiding an imprisonment charge though. They were impressive. Caring and efficient at the same time. "Can you make sure he gets a couple limbs attached before you leave him there?"

"We will, no worries, we've got him," Corey said.

"Maybe drop him a couple of times along the way though. Don't be too nice," Mimi added.

As they moved him he regarded me gratefully. "It's been real. I'll send you a bunch of signed stuff. It might not square us, but you'll have season tickets for the Wizards too. Well, I guess that's not as good as it was yesterday, since the league might disband, but hey, just in case that doesn't happen."

His gratitude was a little confusing. "Well, thanks."

He laughed, picking up on that, I guess. "Seriously, you could have left me behind to get blown up. Darman was one crazy bugger, he was just looking for an excuse to wipe out every officer below him because he couldn't handle the idea that they might be waiting around for someone to take him out so they could move up to the top. I hope he went down with his crappy ship. Sorry about Bergio though."

The medical techs and the security officer stiffened, and with a more serious demeanour the security guard asked; "Permission to debark, Captain?"

Word was spreading about me fast. I hadn't decided whether I liked the reputation I was earning, but I didn't enjoy seeing strangers want to put distance between themselves and me. "Permission granted. Thanks for coming so quickly," I replied. "Take him home."

Synchron barely had time to wave his stump and say; "See ya!" as they carted him off the ship.

"Go die!" Mimi called after him.

"I will definitely not piss you off in the future," Lat said to her.

We watched the ambulance lift up and leave the hangar. The

doors closed right after it, locking with a resounding clang. There was a message from Themis that directed me to Drop Bay Seven, which was nearby. "Time to get going."

I shouldered the bag I'd filled with the recovery solution I'd made earlier along with a backpack that I put several tools and Bergio's arm into. Lat followed my example, grabbing a strange cylindrical bag with handles at one end and dropping hand-held devices inside. It wasn't so much packing in his case, but looting, and he was quick.

"Wait, can I join your crew too?" Mimi asked, stretching up as she sat on her haunches, which I interpreted as a gesture that meant she wanted to be picked up.

"You're the ship mascot," I replied.

"What's a mascot?" Mimi asked as I zipped my jacket up a little, picked her up and put her inside. She had just enough room to ride in there and settled in.

"It's like a lucky charm that makes everyone aboard feel better because you're around," I replied.

"I like that," Mimi said. "I'm lucky."

CHAPTER SIXTEEN

Drop Off

There were a few carts in the hangar near the doors leading further into the facility that were like gurneys but without mattresses or safety features. We put the oblong boxes with the Skyl Brothers inside on them and wheeled them into the hallway. I wouldn't call the interior of that spot clean. The reinforced brick walls and floors had stains and burns that told us that some captures didn't go smoothly, even when you were minutes away from turning your bounty in. It made sense. If I were trying to escape from someone who was about to bring me in, I would definitely give it a try when they're transferring me to a cart.

We headed down the hallways, avoiding a small polishing bot that worked at the worn floor even though it really didn't make a difference. Without letting on that I was doing it, I scanned the boxes with my built-in systems and saw that the brothers were still out. I wouldn't trust their life support to last more than another day, but they would make it to the drop off.

On our way through the halls we passed hunters who I guessed just dropped captures off. Most of them carried durable looking straps with buckles on them. Some slung them over their shoulders, another pair kept them around their waists like thick secondary belts over more fashionable refractory space suits. One duo who were in heavy combat armour, carrying their helmets under their arms stopped us in the hall near the lift. "Hey, new here?" one asked in an accent that seemed related to old British, but more twisted.

"First drop off," I admitted, checking their mechanised plate armour out without using my scanners. If they detected them, it could be considered rude, like peeking underneath.

As the fellow who was talking to me spoke, I turned my eyes up to his broad face. Patchy stubble and blotchy pale skin suggested that some of it had been regenerated recently. "You'll need these." He handed me a set of three straps, buckles included. "If your capture gets off the gurney and another hunter has to help you out, you owe them a meal at the Old Union."

"It's pretty embarrassing, seeing your target get free at turn-in," his partner said to Lat as she put her set of belts on his gurney. "Garshen Lock Belts. Never seen anything break free."

"Thank you, but don't you need them?" Lat asked.

Mimi was taking everything in as she poked her head out from my jacket. I looked the pair up. Since I was a tentative Themis Member, I could see part of their profiles. They were Kad and Rul, a married duo who hunted dangerous targets that law enforcement wouldn't touch. They were the ninth most successful hunters in the solar system.

I was seeing a rare side of these two as Kad looked at Mimi

then me with a question on his face. "You may pet me," Mimi said, interpreting him correctly.

Rul answered Lat as Kad removed one of his gauntlets and gently stroked the top of her head. "We've got plenty of straps on the ship. You can't buy them new anymore and fabricators can't make new ones because they're alive. Just drop them in a bucket with one percent glucose and water every week or so, and they'll live forever."

"Thank you," Lat said.

"It's appreciated," I added as I watched Kad playfully rub under Mimi's chin.

I think he was falling in love. "You are adorbs, wish I had a biccy for ya. She treat you nice?"

"It's early yet, and she has a very strange toilet, but I like her so far," Mimi said, making the bounty hunters grin.

I was blushing furiously. "I'm about to trade the ship in, it's outfitted for a race I've never seen before."

"Been there," Kad slid his gauntlet back on and it clamped to the wrist of his armour loudly. "That's Rul and I'm Kad. Only been here for a few weeks, but I think we're staying."

"This is Mimi," I replied. "That's Lat, I'm Rogue."

Rul nodded at me when my name came up. "Heard about you. Good job on breaking the Darmen up. Why didn't you stay with the wreck and stack plat?"

I was a little confused, but I interpreted the lingo with a guess instead of looking it up. "You mean, salvage the Darmen One? I was in a hurry, and this is my whole crew."

"Ah, that'll answer the question of the day back at the Union," Kad said.

I looked the Old Union up, using my new wrist computer as a proxy connection. It was once the headquarters for the Dock Worker's Union, which represented practically every ground crew member in New Zero over a century ago. Since the unions were dissolved decades ago, it became a popular spot for freelance law enforcement and some of the rougher spacers. "I'll have to drop in sometime. Thank you again for the straps."

"No worries. Good hunting," Kad said as they started moving on. He gave Mimi a parting wink.

"Bye!" she called after them.

"Are all hunters that nice?" she asked.

"I doubt it, but I'm guessing everyone here is pretty happy. This is where they get paid," Lat said as we moved on to the lift.

We went all the way down to sub level fifteen and rolled out into a large waiting room. It was a box with walkways above where soldiers in heavy mechanised armour kept watch carrying multi-mode rifles. Their white plates had the Goddess printed on their backs. She held a sword, shield, wore a helmet and plate armour over white robes. On one shoulder of the guards' armour was a shield, the other a sword, as though being a part of that organisation gave them power similar to the icon they used to represent them.

The walls and floors were clad in plating that reminded me of battlecruisers, and there were no chairs in this waiting room. It wasn't too busy, there were only three lines with five people in them. Many looked over their shoulders at us, and there was a nervous buzz amongst a few as they returned their attention to what they were doing.

At first I thought my work with Darmen had beat me into the room, and maybe it did, but they weren't excited to see me. They were stunned to see Lat. A few of the hunters knew exactly what a Framework Order of Eden soldier looked like, and none had ever seen one who wasn't on the leash.

A man in a full suit of medium plate armour, helmet

included, left his partner in line and walked right up to Lat. His armoured finger poked him. "You don't belong here, war mutt!"

I moved to Lat's side and was just in time to put my hand on his as it touched his sidearm. He looked into my eyes and I could see the fear and aggression there. Before I could say anything, a voice boomed from above. "Conflict during turn in will result in suspension from this and all other Themis Chapters and forfeiture of all bounty rewards."

The man in white armour backed off and started walking towards the main doors behind us, still pointing at Lat. "I see that face out there and I'll make it disappear, asshole!"

Lat ground his teeth and watched. "I liked the wastes better."

"You're all right?" I asked, aware that Mimi's eyes were as round as saucers.

"I'm not injured," he replied.

That, and seeing that he was calming down, was as good as it would get, so I returned to my gurney. "What was that about?" Mimi asked.

"Lat looks like a type of soldier that the Order of Eden uses to attack people," I explained, hoping that she wouldn't follow it up with a series of questions.

She spared me at the moment, but I would have to explain the whole origin and role of the Order in the galaxy a few nights later. While we were in line she was more interested in offering a solution, but only to me in a whisper. "I've seen Bergio do face alterations. They don't hurt, and I bet there's someone else around who can help Lat."

"We'll talk to him about it later," I replied.

One of the only one of the captives was awake and alert. "I am an Islani Count! Your laws don't apply to me! I demand that you release me immediately!"

He struggled in his restraint seat for a moment before the man holding the handles from behind pressed a button and made the Count jerk. "More yap, more zap, Count hoity-toity."

I laughed and the bounty hunter looked over his shoulder. Some of his hair was tied in a top-knot, the rest hung down to his collar. "Guy keeps on forgetting that he's wanted for murdering his own brother. The bounty's set by his government, so it's their laws that got him here. Amazing how he's got this selective memory," he said. "Name's Duncan."

I liked his accent, which reminded me of older Irish English from ancient Earth dramas. "Rogue, this is Mimi," I said, looking down to where she was poking her head out of my jacket.

"Hello," she said.

"Why, you're a pretty one. Pleasure to meet you, Mimi," he said, winking at me.

"Lat," he said, offering his hand stiffly.

"Good to make your acquaintance. I'd shake mitts, but I've gotta keep my hands on the handles," Duncan said, glancing at the Count. A pair of doors at the head of the line parted and the red light over it turned green. "I'm up. Here we go, Count. I get paid, and you get put in a tube until your family can pick you up."

"Please! I have money! I can make you rich!" The Count's begging was accompanied by tears as he struggled to make eye contact with Duncan, who was deaf to his pleas as he was pushed into the room. The doors closed behind them and we moved up in line.

"I liked him, he seemed nice," Mimi said.

Lat leaned back and whispered; "I wouldn't be so quick to trust anyone here."

That brought conversation to a halt. Lat had a talent for

that. We looked around at the hunters who, like us, used carts to move their captures. Most of them weren't in boxes. I was the most lightly armoured there, everyone else at least had plated boots and chest pieces.

One of them, a woman who had a masked human capture strapped down on her cart, was wearing a second skin suit that reminded me of the neck to toe vacsuits that Haven Fleet used. There was a full set of high tech plate armour overtop with dents, scratches and burns that told me that she'd seen some serious combat. I wanted to scan her so I could find out what kind of under suit she was wearing and look up the armour, but I didn't.

I hoped she'd found somewhere selling the multi-layered type of vacsuit that was common in the Haven System. Most spacers, law enforcement and military used them because they didn't get in the way, had multiple layers that each improved the suit's capabilities, and most of them could be adjusted to look like regular clothing. Still, scanning people without a reason was kinda rude, and I was pretty sure she'd probably detect it. "It's Haven Tech," she said, turning towards me so I could see her eyes through the narrow strip of transparent metal in her helmet.

"The armour?" I asked.

"The undersuit. High grade Vacsuit. They just started selling 'em. This batch didn't make it off the docks before they sold out. I've got a guy there, otherwise I would have missed it. You leave your armour on your ship?" she asked.

"It wasn't worth wearing once I was done with it," I replied.

"I'm Cruz. Is that a Violator Seven?"

"Yeah," I replied, aware that Mimi was taking in every word. I don't think she'd ever been outside of Bergio's apartment.

"Hang on to that. The Mark Nine jams, Mark Elevens are

over powered to the point that you need enhancements to shoot it without breaking your forearm, and the new model may never come out. Spectral Dynamics is more interested in overpriced starships and power armour."

"Is that what you're using?" I asked, looking at the chest and arm plates.

"Mostly. Look me up if you want an under suit, I'll have my guy put you on the list," she said as the doors ahead of her parted and the light turned green. "That's me."

"She was scary," Mimi said quietly.

"I bet she's nice when she takes the armour off," I whispered back.

"If she ever takes the armour off," Lat said under his breath.

The doors parted ahead of us and we moved into the room beyond. There was more than enough space for our carts and us. They closed behind and a part of the wall ahead slid up to reveal another layer of metal that was transparent with a non-human behind it. It had a flat head and a narrow neck with big eyes that looked us all over in an instant. She sounded bored as she ground the words in her throat on their way into the air. "Rogue. Delivering Yabrik Skyl and Hovan Skyl, cyborgs. You seem intact, congratulations. Most first time hunters who pursue cyborgs are made into paste or slaves. Cyborgs like them are awful, they fight like idiots, with fists and big bashers so they can feel bones break. Wait for the scan."

We waited as she nodded at a display we couldn't see. "Does everything check out?" Lat asked after a long moment.

"State their condition upon capture," the creature behind the barrier said, ignoring him.

"Well, one doesn't have a head, but his brain wasn't..." I started to explain, not looking forward to going through the list of injuries they'd suffered.

"Alive or dead?" she clarified impatiently.

"Alive," I replied.

"Congratulations, they made it here in the same state. Payment." As she said the word my communications unit blinked, showing that a hundred thousand credits had been transferred to my Fi-Bank account. That was a little over twenty thousand platinum.

"Use the slot." She pointed a long, blue skinned finger with five joints down and to the left. "One at a time."

Lat slid the box with Yabrik inside into the rectangular slot and then I did the same with Hovan. It closed and a door to her right opened. "Go through."

It felt like something was unfinished, like I should be filling a form out or something, and I regarded her awkwardly. "So... there's nothing else..."

"Thank you for all your hard work, hunter. Please go through the door and depart," she said, rolling her big eyes. "Your ranking has been updated."

After going down a straight hallway that was much cleaner than the others, we entered a large lounge with seating in the middle and booths all around. Lat's gaze darted everywhere, and he wandered off to a seller near us who was showing a glittery jumpsuit to Cruz.

I noticed the rankings board, looming large above the vendors on the wall. It featured the top one hundred hunters. Duncan Willow was number ninety-two, which was pretty impressive considering I wasn't on the board at all. As I got closer to it, the large display painted on the wall scrolled down until my name was highlighted on the eight hundred fifty fourth place. "Well, at least I'm not down in the two thousands," I said with a shrug as I joined Lat.

"At the bottom. There are only two thousand-fifty spots and

most of the people down there are dead," Lat clarified as he scrolled to the bottom.

"I got that, thanks," I replied.

"There are that many bounty hunters around?" Mimi asked, surprised.

"Looks like," I replied. I listened in on the obese salesman's pitch as he held a shiny suit out for Cruz to get a closer look.

"What does it do, exactly?" she asked, her voice still distorted slightly by her helmet.

"Well, we're raising funds for another round of research so it can do exactly what we're proposing," he explained. "With your investment..."

"So, it doesn't do anything yet," Cruz said, stepping back. "What do you want it to do?"

"Well, that's not true. Right now it efficiently disintegrates whoever wears and activates it. That only means that we're that much closer to true functionality. This suit will be able to teleport you across a solar system, or with enough power, the galaxy," he said as though it was a great revelation.

"Amazing. The strategic significance of teleportation is very high," Lat said.

Cruz walked away. "I have credits to spend, but not here."

Mimi's laughter pierced the air, shrill and full bodied. I could feel her shaking. "Teleportation of that type requires the annihilation of the subject in one place and the creation of an exact duplicate in another. It's foolish! Pure energy fabricators at the highest level are too large and complicated to fit into a suit, and if they did, it would be better to just copy yourself so you can be in two places at once!"

"But, we believe that someone can be transmitted using..."

"Farce! Foolishness!" she shrieked. Then she calmed down and looked up at me. "Can we go?"

The researcher stared on, agape, lowering the suit slowly. "I've been disparaged by a Kawaii Kitten," he muttered.

"Okay," I said, a little astonished too. There was obviously a lot I didn't know about Mimi.

"Keep trying," Lat whispered to him as we moved on.

The three of us walked past a few booths selling equipment and offering services. "The list is probably for the whole solar system. I'm surprised too though, Themis hasn't been operating long."

"So, we work for them now?" Lat asked.

"No, we're mercenaries. We can take jobs from anyone. There are other bounty boards, this is just the one that seems most organised. They definitely have their security and procedures wired up right from the looks of it. They also have a huge list of normal things for people to do, you know, stuff that doesn't require firepower."

"Oh, so what are we doing next? What's the next job?" Lat asked.

"We have to get a few things sorted before we take anything on. I've got two thirds of a ship to claim and we're moving into the Envoy," I replied. He needed to keep busy. I spotted a booth with a grey haired Obrun wearing goggles and a jumpsuit behind it. The name of their company was Jekker Yards, and I stepped in front of them. "You deal in used ships?"

"Yes, what do you want to sell me?" she asked, idly running her claws - which were painted shiny blue - through the fur under her chin.

"You buy ships from hunters?" Lat asked.

"Ships, what's inside the ships, you know, all the things," she replied.

I brought up the scan results for the Hinow-Sa and sent

them to the terminal built into the front of the booth. "There's a whole cyborg workshop in there."

"Nice scans, very clear, very complete. The guy in the closet come with it?" she asked with a chuckle.

"Oh, no, That scan was taken before he was sent home," I replied.

She waved my explanation off as she looked the scans over. "No judgement, you couldn't imagine the messed up wrecks hunters sell me, you know. Oh, I see, fully functional. Upgraded weapon system, too bad the missile launchers are empty. You're right, there's a lot of good stationary equipment there. The tools aren't worth anything, the fabricators are basic models, but they're new. Obuudain fixtures? Oh, no. Someone's taken a perfectly good - if basic - ship and installed an Obuudain kit."

"You mean the bathroom?" Mimi asked.

"The bathroom, the living quarters, the bridge, even the escape pods. There might be ten of those ugly Obuudains in the solar system, and I'm sure none of them are interested in an entry level ship like this. Do you still have the biped support kit in storage somewhere?"

"No, sorry," I replied.

"Well. We're going to have to make one to sell this ship, that'll cut into the offer I can make. The equipment in the hold is good though, and that car is nice, we can build it up like a hot rod and turn that around," she said before taking a moment to consider.

I looked up a few ship trade sites on my wrist, sending the scans into their estimators and didn't like the quotes that were coming back. She was right. People wanted ships with bipedal bathrooms, chairs and beds. "So, will you take it?"

"You're new, and you've made a big splash on your first time out, so sure. I'll give you twenty-three thousand for all of it. We're going to have to do a lot of work before it's sold."

That was low. Very low. "Okay, you're not doing me a favour at that price."

She laughed and pointed at my bracer. "So you were shopping around on that thing, I thought so. Do you have the command chip?"

I fished it out of my bra, a little embarrassed that I hadn't taken a minute to print a chain for it, then held it up. "It's registered under my Ident. There's a minor conflict, maybe."

She accepted it, put it into a reader on her wrist and waited. Then she ejected it, blew on the slot, the chip and did it again. The registration came up and she said; "Not seeing a conflict that matters here, so that makes you the owner. That changes things. You didn't collect this as a bounty though, so I'm not getting subsidisation from Tabrus or New Zero. Can't give you as much, it's practically a found ship," she said, scratching her chin.

"What's a found ship?" Mimi asked.

"It's when the dirtbag using it is killed and someone better at filling forms out claims it more legitimately. Happens a lot around here. Okay, forty thousand Themis Credits since your name is on that chip and the Navnet registration," she offered.

The highest quote I got online was fifty-eight, but I would have to fly it to a station near the edge of the solar system to cash that in. "Fifty and you have a deal," I said.

"With the car?" Lat asked.

"With the car," the Obrun said. "And it's forty-five thousand. You won't get better around here. That is, unless you're willing to throw in the kitty. I'll give you five thousand for her."

"No sale, sorry," I replied, stroking Mimi's head. Her jaw had dropped. She stared at the Obrun, shocked.

"I had to try. All right, forty-five thousand it is."

"If your guys pick it up from the Themis dock," I told her.

"Absolutely," she replied, placing the chip on a small tablet sitting on the counter between us. "Just transfer ownership and you'll get forty five grand in your account. Use this terminal."

I did so, watching the offer come up. As soon as I transferred ownership, Fi-Bank sent me a message telling me that I was forty-five thousand Themis Credits richer. "Thank you," I said, waiting for her to give me her name.

"Kambla," she said. "Anytime. Check us out if you need a nice reconditioned ship. Our dock is in orbit and we keep a full inventory list with virtual tours online."

"I might," I replied. Feeling a few hundred tons lighter, we moved on, ignoring the rest of the booths in the large lounge court.

EPILOGUE

When People Keep Their Word

We moved on to the Envoy, where it landed in my rented hangar. Lat and Mimi had never seen anything like the luxury ship. As they admired the real wood floors decorating the lounging area, the high-end food fabricators and automatically adjusting seating throughout, I decided not to tell them that it was technically a stolen ship according to the Order of Eden. If they ever got a foothold on Tabrus so they could enforce their laws, I would be wanted for Grand Theft Starship. It would have to go one way or another, and it was too small for what I was planning with accommodations for three crew members and power systems that were already maxed out.

The thought of going on a search for a new ship was exciting, and I looked forward to either digging one up or buying one. Used or new didn't matter. What I wanted would have to be military grade at its core, big enough for a crew of seven, but small enough to go just about anywhere. It would take time, luck and maybe wealth to find that.

Before anyone was finished exploring, the remains of the Uwebo were delivered. As soon as it was carefully placed beside the Envoy by a tug that held the main body of the ship with massive grippers, there was a transfer to my Fi-Bank account. Two hundred ten thousand credits, which came out to forty-five thousand seven hundred eighty platinum with the exchange rate at the time. I told him I wanted to be paid in plat, but I wouldn't make a big deal about getting paid in Tabrus Credits, especially since that was the only part of the deal he broke.

As soon as the Uwebo was settled on the deck, the tug took off. There was no dramatic meeting, not even a conversation. I was suspicious and checked the contents of the ship's remains right away. The door that I was flung through earlier was patched hastily but effectively, keeping everything inside as they moved it from space to my hangar.

My bike, the box of credits, even the case of guns I had stashed away were still in there along with every crate and other odd item that didn't get tossed into space when I made my hasty exit. There were components, like the backup life support and wormhole compression modules that I'd hang on to. The rest would be pushed aside for spare parts or to be sold as scrap if the demand went up. I found Nera's personal computer in a little box with a bow on it on one of the two bunks inside the Uwebo.

There was a buzz after my name hit the bounty boards. The community didn't know what to think of me coming in with such a big capture. My deal with Vasard and the thank you note I sent him after earned me a positive comment from him online.

. . .

Rogue is a straight shooter. You don't have to wait around for her to tell you what she wants, and our deal was pretty fair. Don't steal a pip from this chick though, she'll hunt you down and make you regret it.

My profile was littered with comments from people who I'd never met who looked at my friendly headshot and immediately rendered judgements. Most of them were spectators, hunter chasers, who had a voracious appetite for takedown footage and rooted for one bounty hunter or another. They argued that I didn't look like a serious hunter, or they came at it from the other end, saying that you could never tell what someone was capable of from their profile images. There were a lot of more crude, insulting comments, but I filtered those out right away. The few hunters who commented had a more 'wait and see' attitude, since I was so new. I decided not to let any of that get to me, but looking back on it now, I know it did, and the doubt that the public had in me got in my head more than I'd like to admit.

It, and several other factors, would change things soon after, and my hunting tactics would eventually get even more ruthless. Not right away, though, I had a crew of two to look after, and I was determined to provide for them without putting them in direct danger, at least not until I knew what they could handle.

I wanted to be the white knight at the beginning of this journey, but complications and experience would darken my tactics before long. I'd like to finish this log on a happy note, so the details of my bounty hunting career after the Darmen Corporation fell will have to wait. It's a longer story than I have time for at the moment.

As for the problem that led me to Bergio for help, well, I'll always be grateful to him for helping me look inward. After finding that I had a bio-brain and a digi-brain in my chest the problem was bigger. I needed to find someone who could build a new cooling solution so I wouldn't fry my bio-brain if my computer ran faster than thirty-three percent of its maximum speed. I still didn't trust anyone - even Haven Sciences, the place that could make androids just like me, to crack the layers of armour in my chest so they could tinker around. I didn't have the skills to fix it myself using nanobots, and telling someone about the problem would probably mean showing them a schematic of my inner workings. I wasn't ready to do that either.

So, until I get that solution somewhere - whether I figure it out or commission some genius to do it - I'm limited. The good thing about that is that I get to feel more like myself, so unless I need to do some fast Stellarnet browsing or hard math, I kept that computer running nice and cool, lower than thirty-three percent. I would like to know what it's like to experience my full digital capacity while my more human side - the bio-brain - isn't getting fried though. Maybe someday.

Okay, let's look at some bigger picture stuff. The Ballistic Crush League was in crisis, so the Tabrus Government nationalised it at the last moment, taking full control. They put the current season on pause so a new board could convene, reformatting the sport so it was a little slower with a goal post at either end of a larger oval field with obstacles. They sold the teams off. Siren Arms bought The New Zero Wizards, and I got a surprise delivery a week later from Synchron. It was a box filled with new merchandise along with a pair of season tickets.

The sport grew on me, but I created a monster when I watched a few old matches with Lat. He was an instant super fan. Apparently Synchron did some thinking while he was in the closet and, as he said in a few interviews, "Realised the true value and importance of life." In a tell-all series of viral videos, he shared how Nera, representing the Darmen Corporation, kept him hopped up on the drugs of his choice as she had people sell what he called; 'Celebrity Time' with him to only the highest paying fans. Free from her and the Darmen Corp, he was substance free, better than ever on the field, and working with his favourite charity, Orphans Of The Fall.

He never mentioned me by name, but said he owed his new turn in life to the one who took Nera and the Darmen Corporation out of the picture. Everyone in the hunter community and corporate culture knew it was me.

Themis quickly became the largest Justice Management Company in the solar system, even though they were simply a middle man, setting hunters up with targets that were vetted by a fast, strict legal system as well as non-violent shipping, fetching and other jobs that paid a fair industry rate. They added their modest finder fee to everything, and most big entities like governments and corporations were happy to pay it because going through them meant that they didn't have to find their own hunters and jobbers. Limited liability is preferred for most governments, regardless if things are made better or worse.

Siren Arms filed a purchase offer for the largest continent on Tabrus and it went through in seven days. Critics still attack the Tabrus government for making the deal, calling them out for greed, and they attack Siren Arms for bribing every governor on the planet. It's history now, though, since Siren Arms owns a huge land mass, becoming the governing body there. They took the opportunity to rename their corporation simply 'Siren' and the continent after its founder, the enigmatic Surbane. I still don't know where I stand on that. I like watching companies compete as long as war doesn't break out, so I hope Siren doesn't turn into another oppressive corp. The good news is that they're selling assets, like my hangar, so I may not have to rent forever if I decide to stay.

Mimi enjoyed the Envoy right away, claiming a corner of the Captain's Quarters, where I sometimes napped; my Bio-brain still needs sleep. I kept those quarters for the storage space, not for the huge bed or nice fixtures. Mimi got her fine bed and had all her things around it, but rarely used it since she could nap on my bed whenever she wanted.

I'd like to say that Lat changed after he took that pill, that there was some kind of great drama surrounding the event. It would be good for the story, but I'm happy to say that he took the thing, got rid of the Framework after a quick regeneration and woke up looking exactly as he did before, only about ten centimetres taller. Now he towers over me and hits his head on his way into the bathroom sometimes. That always gets a good laugh from Mimi.

What about me? Well, over the days following the fall of the Darmen Corporation, I thought about Bergio a lot. He helped me literally look within myself so I could re-scan my systems and find a temporary fix for my Bio-Brain and computerised mind. The balance still isn't right, I need to figure out a fix for that or find someone I trust enough to make modifications to the most important part of my body, but I feel better.

Bergio also showed me that you really could cut ties and start over. He made leaving an old life behind look easy, and I considered that a lot since Alice's life, filled with amazing people, wasn't mine to touch. Or was it? More than ever, I didn't feel like I was just a copy anymore. I think about Jacob Valent, and feel closer to him because when he didn't know where he came from, who his people were, or what he ought to do, he became a hunter. All he had was a gun, a ship, and a need to keep going. That felt like my road.

When Lat took the pill that removed the Framework System from his body, I made good on my promise. I considered calling Alice, of course, that would be the easiest one. Then I scrolled through the list of people who had called me, looking at all the names, and as I was looking at Jake's number, he called. I answered, about as nervous as I think anyone could be.

At first he looked stunned. I'd ignored three calls from him so far, and I'm guessing he expected to leave a message for me like he'd done before. Then he broke into a smile and said; "Congratulations, I saw your name on the Themis Hunter Board."

Shocked, I replied; "Thanks. You saw that? You're a member?"

"I was signed up under a different Themis Chapter for a while, so I stay up to date. A hunter never stops checking the boards," he replied. "Are you all right out there?"

"Good, I'm good." Projected by the system in my room, his holographic head was staring at me, and I wondered if he was already struggling for something to say. Then, I realised that Bergio may have shown me how he could cut ties and leave everything behind, but that didn't mean I could. It didn't mean I should.

I loved Jake like a true daughter looking up to her father, and it felt different from the affection Alice had for him. It's not easy to explain, but let's say that I felt the potential for a kinship. He filled the silence while I started to smile at him. "I was going to leave you a message, give you a head's up about Haven Fleet entering talks with Themis so they can extend the bounties on Order of Eden, Citadel, the Edxi and every other target on their list to your area. It looks like Themis will be honouring our bounties sometime in the next few weeks."

"Are there targets out here?" I asked. The idea of having

Order and Citadel bounties near New Zero and a place to drop them off outside of the Haven System was thrilling.

"I can't go into specifics, but our intelligence says so. Think you'll keep hunting?" Jake asked.

"Definitely," I replied. "I might take a break from cyborgs though."

"I lost a lot of hardware going after Street Metal," Jake said, nodding. "They're expensive targets."

"Oh, brutally," I laughed.

"Need anything?" he asked.

I could have asked for a lot just then, but I've got this problem where I want to earn what I own, so I didn't request gear, or backup. I went another way instead. "I could use a few pointers, if you have the time."

"I've got the time," he replied.

That was the beginning of our real relationship. I wasn't ready to talk to anyone else from Alice's life, so he kept our chats a secret, but I felt like a daughter again, and we were talking about more than hunting before long.

AFTERWORD

Rogue Is Assembled

Cyborgs, Nera, bounty hunting and a new sport. These are the things that came about last for this book. The idea of a Kawaii Kitten has been around for a while in the Spinward Fringe Series, and I considered putting one in Psycho Electric, but it didn't seem appropriate.

With every good adventure, there are a few laughs and some unexpected whimsy. Mimi is my whimsy cat, and I hope you enjoyed seeing the first characterised Kawaii Kitten arrive in the Spinward Fringe Universe. Writing scenes with her, Lat and Rogue was like having three very distinct voices in my head, and there were scenes where Synchron made it a quartet. I admit, there was a moment when he was almost invited onto the crew, but he wounded everyone else too deeply by leading Nera and the Darmen Corporation to Bergio. In the end I liked the idea of his experience with Rogue making him a better cyborg.

Now, let's get serious for a minute. Since 1977 I've been

looking for more stories about gunslingers, bounty hunters and other colourful characters in science fiction. There have been fantastic shows, movies and books around since then, but I've never thought it was enough. After Rogue made her first appearance at the end of Hunters: Spinward Fringe Broadcast 16, I started wondering what her story would be. What would she do after the wastes of Tabrus were tamed? Would she go on to fight the Order? Was she doing that already?

Well, the simple answer was that she was working against the Order of Eden, the current big bad organisation in the main Spinward Fringe Series, but she'd run into a couple of complications. They're detailed in this book. You know; personality balance, potential technical difficulties, a real need to avoid a direct confrontation because she was alone, and the fact that androids aren't allowed to pretend they're human in most civilisations. All that makes fighting the Order a little hard. Besides, I wanted her to have her own origin story after her creation on Rodus in the Hunters novel. When I realised that she could be my sci-fi gunslinger, I knew I had the right ideas for a book I'd enjoy. It was time for me to add my own voice to that sub-sub genre again, and if it became a series, that would be the core of it.

That's what this book is. It's how she becomes more than the sum of her parts, brings her first crew member on, and adopts the ship pet. Oh, and she becomes a mercenary. The decision to have her get in touch with Jacob Valent came on the last day. I hadn't decided until then, and it almost went to a vote amongst my Ream Stories readers, but I ran out of time. After it was written I loved it.

There's so much more I could say about this novel, but I think the most important thing is that I really enjoyed writing it. Even though a third of these chapters were written, scrapped and then written again, it was an exciting ride for me. So much so that I wanted to go on to write the next one a day later, but I'm taking a break to write an epic about star fighter pilots next. It's like going from guilty pleasure to guilty pleasure, but I don't hear anyone complaining.

Regardless of how successful this short novel is, I'll be writing two more that will be around the same size. Look for Rogue to return in 2024 or early 2025 in Rogue Cause.

CREDITS

I'm grateful to Heather Berlekamp and Janet Lalonde for leading the charge in proofreading Rogue Assembly. They make me look good and give you a better reading experience.

Thank you to the Ream Readers for your support and help in proofreading. They are:

Alan
> *Charles Ferguson*
> *Charles Love*
> *Dave James*
> *Paul Gear*
> *Joe L Goode*
> *Jac Grimes*
> *John Hawker*
> *Lorie Holmed*
> *Art Jenkins*

Gene Martin
Jeff Mueller
Tom
Enforcer83
Smilinjeff03

SPINWARD FRINGE UNIVERSE TIMELINE

With regard to the Rogue Element series, Psycho Electric and The Last of the Bullet Chasers, you don't have to read any of the other Spinward Fringe novels to understand and enjoy them. You can also read Carnie's Tale and The Expendable Few separately if you'd rather dip your toe into the universe than start at the beginning with Spinward Fringe Broadcast 0: Origins. Having said that, if you're going to dive into the series, and I invite you to, it's a hell of a ride, here is the chronological order of all the books in the Spinward Fringe Universe.

Spinward Fringe Broadcast 0: Origins
Spinward Fringe Broadcast 1 and 2: Resurrection and Awakening
Spinward Fringe Broadcast 3: Triton
Spinward Fringe Broadcast 4: Frontline
Spinward Fringe Broadcast 5: Fracture
Spinward Fringe Broadcast 6: Fragments
The Expendable Few: A Spinward Fringe Novel
Spinward Fringe Broadcast 7: Framework

Spinward Fringe Broadcast 8: Renegades
Spinward Fringe Broadcast 9: Warpath
Trapped: Chaos Core Book 1
Cool Pursuit: Chaos Core Book 2
Spinward Fringe Broadcast 10: Freeground
Spinward Fringe Broadcast 10.5: Carnie's Tale
Spinward Fringe Broadcast 11: Revenge
Savage Stars: Chaos Core Book 3
Spinward Fringe Broadcast 12: Invasion
Spinward Fringe Broadcast 13: Warriors
Spinward Fringe Broadcast 14: Rebel
Spinward Fringe Broadcast 15: Pursuit
Spinward Fringe Broadcast 16: Hunters
Psycho Electric - A Spinward Fringe Novel
The Last of the Bullet Chasers - A Spinward Fringe Short
Novella
Spinward Fringe Broadcast 17: Clash
Spinward Fringe Broadcast 18: Samurai Squadron
Spinward Fringe Broadcast 19: Samurai Squadron II
Rogue:Assembly
Rogue Cause
Rogue Chase (2025)
Spinward Fringe Broadcast 20: Samurai Squadron III
Legion: Spinward Fringe Broadcast 21 (Late 2025)

THE FANTASY NOVELS

With regards to the Rogue Element series, Psycho Electric and The Last of the Bullet Chasers, you don't have to read any of the other Spinward Fringe novels to understand and enjoy them. You can also read Carnie's Tale and The Expendable Few separately if you'd rather dip your toe into the universe than start at the beginning with Spinward Fringe Broadcast 0: Origins. Having said that, if you're going to dive into the series, and I invite you to, it's a hell of a ride, here is the chronological order of all the books in the Spinward Fringe Universe.

Spinward Fringe Broadcast 0: Origins

Spinward Fringe Broadcast 1 and 2: Resurrection and Awakening

Spinward Fringe Broadcast 3: Triton

Spinward Fringe Broadcast 4: Frontline

Spinward Fringe Broadcast 5: Fracture

Spinward Fringe Broadcast 6: Fragments

The Expendable Few: A Spinward Fringe Novel

Spinward Fringe Broadcast 7: Framework

Spinward Fringe Broadcast 8: Renegades

Spinward Fringe Broadcast 9: Warpath

Trapped: Chaos Core Book 1

Cool Pursuit: Chaos Core Book 2

Spinward Fringe Broadcast 10: Freeground

Spinward Fringe Broadcast 10.5: Carnie's Tale

Spinward Fringe Broadcast 11: Revenge

Savage Stars: Chaos Core Book 3

Spinward Fringe Broadcast 12: Invasion

Spinward Fringe Broadcast 13: Warriors

Spinward Fringe Broadcast 14: Rebel

Spinward Fringe Broadcast 15: Pursuit

Spinward Fringe Broadcast 16: Hunters

Psycho Electric - A Spinward Fringe Novel

The Last of the Bullet Chasers - A Spinward Fringe Short Novella

Spinward Fringe Broadcast 17: Clash

Spinward Fringe Broadcast 18: Samurai Squadron

Spinward Fringe Broadcast 19: Samurai Squadron II

Rogue:Assembly
Rogue Cause
Rogue Chase (2025)
Spinward Fringe Broadcast 20: Samurai Squadron III
Legion: Spinward Fringe Broadcast 21 (Late 2025)

THE FANTASY NOVELS

While most of these aren't arranged into a series, they do land
on a timeline and occur in the world of Nemori. Here's the
chronological order of all my fantasy novels, which are written to
be enjoyed in any order except for the NEM novels.

Brightwill
Highshield
NEM: Awakening
NEM: Crimson Shores

While most of these aren't arranged into a series, they do land
on a timeline and occur in the world of Nemori. Here's the
chronological order of all my fantasy novels, which are written to
be enjoyed in any order except for the NEM novels.

Brightwill
Highshield
NEM: Awakening
NEM: Crimson Shores

WHERE YOU CAN FIND ME AND OTHER STORIES.

If you'd like more information about me, to get in touch, read articles or find out what's going on you can visit my website at www.randolphlalonde.com or www.spinwardfringe.com. If you'd like to access my entire library, including a couple exclusives starting in 2024, and read the newest books before release in a serialised format, please visit my Ream Stories site: https://ream stories.com/randolphlalonde